A, MY NAME IS
Ami

Look for these other books
about best friends
by NORMA FOX MAZER:

B, My Name Is Bunny
C, My Name Is Cal
D, My Name Is Danita
E, My Name Is Emily

A, MY NAME IS
Ami

NORMA FOX MAZER

AN
APPLE
PAPERBACK

SCHOLASTIC INC.
New York Toronto London Auckland Sydney

ISBN 0-590-43896-4

Copyright © 1986 by Norma Fox Mazer.
All rights reserved. Published by Scholastic Inc.
APPLE PAPERBACKS is a registered trademark of Scholastic Inc.

14 13 12 11 10 9 8 7 6 5 4 3   4 5 6 7 8 9/9

Printed in the U.S.A.   40

For Barbara Karlin —
old friends when we first met

A, MY NAME IS
Ami

Chapter 1

My brother knocked on the door while I was in the shower, "Ami, get out of there," he yelled.

I poked my head around the shower curtain. "Can't you wait a few more minutes?"

"No! I've got a zit, and Jan's coming over." Fred banged on the door again. "Ami! Are you looking to make it into the *Guinness Book of Records*? Do you really mean to spend the best years of your life in the shower? I'm warning you, you are going to end up with old, wrinkled alligator skin from all that water."

Fred is like Dad. He can talk — and talk, and talk, and talk. I don't talk that much, maybe that's why I like the shower. I do some of my best thinking in there. It's an actual fact that running water relaxes you. It has something to

1

do with the water producing all these little negative ions that go charging around in the air and which, even though they're negative, are terrifically good for you.

If I have a terrible problem, even if I feel like all I want to do is scream, or get in bed and never wake up, I can stand under the shower and, after a while, not feel so awful. The night my mother went away in May was like that. I was running the water so hard, nobody even knew I was crying. If I was ever going to get alligator skin from showering, that was the night. The whole bathroom must have been loaded up with negative ions. I stood there so long, the water turned ice cold.

"Ami!" Fred was back again. "Phone."

"Is this a trick?"

"Would I do that? Your clone is on the phone."

I hopped out of the shower and pulled on my pj's and robe. "Who?"

"Your spiritual twin. Your other self."

"It's Mia?"

"Is that a description of anybody else? Come to think of it, does anybody else call you?"

I opened the door. "Very funny, Freddy. Ha ha. Oh! You do have a zit." He pushed past me and slammed the door.

Fred is sensitive about his complexion. He's five years older than I am, on the short, skinny side and — though I would never tell him, since

2

he thinks well enough of himself already — he is really cute. He dresses preppy, has lots of dark hair, and a great smile. You can see that smile gleaming out in his yearbook pictures. In the photo of the French Club, also known as Le Club, all eleven members (not exactly the biggest club in Jefferson High) are sitting around a table, smiling, but Fred's smile outshines them all.

I ran downstairs. "Hello, Mia," I said, picking up the phone in the kitchen.

"Ami! At last! Where were you? I've been waiting for you to call me. Don't you remember what today is?"

"I remember, Mia. I was going to call."

"I was going crazy! I thought you'd forgotten. If you forgot, I was going to kill you, personally!"

Dad says that Mia always sounds like she's either won the lottery or lost a fortune. "That girl is either shrieking or groaning." It is true that Mia can be sort of excessive, but it's just that, to her, every little thing in life is exciting.

I remember, once, we were taking a walk and turned down a side street. A lot of little houses, then suddenly a tiny storefront in one of the houses, with a crayoned sign in the window. HOMEMADE ICE CREAM. RELIABLE. Mia got excited right away. "We have to go in, Ami!" A bell tinkled when we opened the door, and an old man with a brown-spotted bald head leaned across the counter.

"We want your reliable ice cream," Mia said.

"Don't sell nothing else here."

"Is it really homemade?"

"Wouldn't sell it if it wasn't." He was so old his hands shook when he dipped the ice cream. "Make it myself every day. Three flavors. Today is vanilla, peach, and raspberry. Come tomorrow, three different flavors."

Mia's eyes were shining. "We'll have one cone of each flavor."

Outside, we passed the cones back and forth. The peach was okay, the raspberry was watery, but the vanilla was awful. It tasted like the medicine my mother used to give us when we had diarrhea.

"Who cares?" Mia said. "*Homemade ice cream*, Ami. That's like finding sunken treasure. It's so rare!" And she made me feel as if finding that place and eating that awful ice cream was a fabulous event in my life. It's a kind of genius she has for making everything special.

"Ami," she said now, intensely, "it's our anniversary."

"I know. October fifteenth. I didn't forget. Happy anniversary, Mia. I was going to call you."

"Happy anniversary, Ami! I knew you'd call, but I just couldn't wait."

Mia and I have been best friends for four years. Everything about us is either just the opposite, or else matches. Our names have the same letters. We each have an older sib — mine's a brother, hers is a sister. I'm more athletic, she's more imaginative. My hair is heavy and hers is sort of bouncy and light. I'm tall, with my deep voice and sort of round face. Mia is small, she just comes up to my shoulder, and her face goes right to a point at her chin.

Even our birthdays match, in a way. Mine is June twenty-first, hers is December third. Two and one (my numbers) make three (her number). Also, our birthdays are the sixth month and the twelfth month, which can both be divided by three, and they're six months apart and six divided by two makes three again. Three is our special number.

Last spring we each inked a triangle on our hands with PAA written around the sides. Three sides. Three letters. PAA. Protection Against Anything. Mia said PAA really worked. She said it was because of PAA that Ronnie and Davis Buck, who are cousins and two of the biggest pains in our class, stopped pestering her so much. Maybe. But PAA didn't stop my mother from leaving us.

Sometimes Mia and I wear the same clothes, like one day we'll both wear red scarves around our necks, or maybe our blue corduroy caps and blue knee socks. We tell each other our dreams, we call each other up and check out what we're watching on TV. And every year, ever since we became friends, we've liked the same boy.

It began in fourth grade with Bruno Morelli.

5

He wore a leather jacket and had beautiful green eyes. First, we both liked him alone and secretly. Then we talked it over and decided to like him together and secretly. We used to follow him home two or three times a week and leave love notes for him in his lunch box or in his desk or his jacket pocket. Once when we went by his house, he'd left his sneakers out on his lawn, and we put a note in each sneaker.

"I made up a poem about Robert," Mia said. "It's not very good — do you want to hear it?"

"Yes."

"It's awful, really."

"Read it to me."

She cleared her throat. " 'To Robert, Who Has Red Hair.' That's the title. 'To Robert, Who Has Red Hair.' "

"I know that's the title."

"It's awful, I better not read it."

"I like the title," I said.

"You do? You're not just saying that?"

"You know me better than that, Mia. Read!"

"Okay, here goes." She cleared her throat again. Then she read, very fast, " 'To Robert, Who Has Red Hair. Your glasses shine like the sun. Your hair is red as rain. Oh Robert, Robert, Robert Volz! To love you is such sweet pain!' "

We both burst out laughing. We couldn't stop. I slid right down on the floor and rolled around with the telephone at my ear.

"It's awful," Mia screamed, laughing, "it's awful, isn't it awful, Ami?"

6

"Well . . . when you say, 'Your hair is red as rain.' Red rain?"

"Poetic license. I'll tear it up."

I sat up. "No, Mia, you have to keep it for the archives."

"Ami, I'd rather throw it away and write something better."

"No way, Mia. You know the rules."

Every year when we like the same boy, we keep a record of anything that has to do with him and us. Mostly, it's a notebook we write in, but sometimes we get some object that belongs to him. The archives are actually just an old cardboard sneaker box where we keep all the stuff. Still, it's part of our tradition.

You have to realize all this about rules and archives started back in fifth grade with Raymond Fuller when we acquired two things of his and had a huge fight, all on the same day. The first thing we got was a blue ballpoint pen he threw away. The second was a wad of chewed-up bubble gum. We dared each other to grab the pen from the wastebasket during recess. Mia finally fished out the pen. "Here, you keep it!" She passed it to me. Later, that same day, we followed Raymond home. About halfway there, he spat out his gum, and I said we should pick it up and keep it with the pen.

Mia said that was a disgusting idea. I said we didn't have to touch the gum. "We'll wrap it up in paper."

"It's still disgusting!"

7

"I thought you said we should keep everything we found of his."

"I meant, like pens," Mia said. "Why do you have to be so *literal*?"

"Why do you have to show off your vocabulary? I know you know biiiig words."

"Oh, excuse me! I'll use little words for your little mind. I. Do. Not. Want. To. Pick. Up. Dirty. Gum!"

We stood on the sidewalk and argued. Raymond was out of sight by now. Secretly I thought Mia was right, but I was too stubborn to admit it. I pointed out to her that she was the one who noticed that Raymond had spit out his gum. "You said it first, Mia. Do you admit you said it first?"

"Do you think you're the district attorney or something, Ami? Did I commit a crime? We just have totally different *values*. I don't see why I'm your friend, *at all*."

"Nobody's forcing you," I said.

We walked in opposite directions, but first I picked up the bubble gum. It was definitely disgusting, but after our fight I couldn't *not* do it. Mia and I were mad at each other for three days. It was the worst fight we'd ever had. And, Mia said, after we made up, the stupidest. That was when we made rules for ourselves. Rule One. *Anything* we find that belongs to the beloved, we keep. Rule Two. *Anything* we write about the beloved, we keep. Rule Three. *All* fights to be made up after a period of no longer than one day.

"The archives!" Mia said now. "The poem has to go in the archives. Oh, no! It's there forever and ever and ever." She sounded very dramatic. "I got carried away, Ami."

"So what else is new?"

"Maybe I could just throw it away this one time?" she wheedled.

"Mia, I didn't make the rules."

"Okay, okay, I'll keep it."

After we talked a while longer, I went up to my room and got into bed with Unccy Bernard. Unccy is a large yellow plush bear that my uncle Bernard sent for me when I was born. Uncle Bernard Lamott is my mother's brother. He has a farm in Wisconsin. I don't really know him, because I've only seen him two times in my life. I guess that's why, when I was a little kid, I got mixed up and thought the bear was my actual uncle, which is how he got his name.

The thing about Unccy Bernard is that there's a place to put your hands and arms inside him from the back, so you can move his head and arms.

I put my hands inside him. "Well, Ami, sweetheart," I had him say, "how're things with you?"

"Oh . . . okay. I had an okay day."

Unccy put big furry yellow paws to his face. "What's the matter, sweetheart?"

"Nothing."

9

"You can tell your old Unccy, darling." Unccy flopped his head against my shoulder. A furry yellow paw patted my face.

"Oh, Unccy — " My throat got sort of thick.

"You going to cry?" Unccy asked. "Unccy doesn't mind." He made little kissing sounds at me. "Unccy doesn't mind if his sweetheart cries."

"No, it's so stupid to cry." I started crying. "See! I'm getting your fur all wet and it's going to s-stink."

Unccy kept his head close to mine. "You want to tell old Unccy what's bothering you?"

"Unccy — it's so hard to say."

"Old Unccy will take a guess." He tapped his forehead. "Thinking, you know." He twisted his head around to look at me. "You're not used to your mom living over there in New Castle. Nod once if Unccy is right."

I nodded once.

"Let Unccy take another guess. You miss her. Nod twice if Unccy is right."

I nodded twice and lay back with Unccy in my arms. I hoped Fred didn't come in and find me like that.

Chapter 2

Last year, right at the end of the term, Mr. Feld, our science teacher, suddenly quit. Nobody knew why. There were rumors. One was that Mr. Feld was going into the paratroopers. Another rumor was that he had punched out Mr. Cooper, the gym teacher. Everybody was excited and then they forgot him. Ms. Linsley took his place. I remember the exact day she came to school. May 21, a Thursday, one month before my birthday, and the day after my mother finally moved out.

About a week after that, Mia got sick with walking pneumonia. You think people get pneumonia in winter, not when it's practically summer. I was really scared the whole time she was sick. I kept thinking, Mom's moved out, now

Mia's sick. Two bad things have happened, what's next?"

Every day after school, I'd go around to the teachers and bring them Mia's work that she was doing at home and see if they wanted me to tell her anything. That's how I got to know Ms. Linsley really well. Her whole name is Forrest Lake Linsley. She's taller than I am, with curly brown hair and really thick, dark eyebrows that almost meet over her nose. One day she told me that she used to hate her eyebrows and tried to pluck them out when she was my age. "But now I let them go their own way. They're me, part of me, you know what I'm saying, Ami?"

I nodded. It's like my voice, which is really deep. Sometimes kids mock me out because of my voice, call me Foghorn Ami, and I feel unhappy. But I can't do anything about it, can I? Some things you can change about yourself, but not your voice.

Ms. Linsley said she had been substitute teaching since she graduated college. This was her first regular job. "You think you're practicing for the real thing," she said, "but when the real thing comes, it's entirely different. It's scary!"

I knew what she meant. For months before that, my mother had been ready to move out of our house, and I had been practicing for when she did it. It started when she and Dad told Fred and me they were going to have a trial separation, to see if they liked living apart better. "Why?" I said.

"Because we need to do this," Mom said. "It happens to people. Listen, when you get married, you want it to be forever and wonderful, but sometimes it — just isn't. You live together and then, at some point, you realize that maybe it isn't the best thing for either of you. Do you see?"

"No," I said, because I didn't.

She hugged me. "Honey, we're just in different places in our lives."

"Sure," Fred said, like he was this superior grown-up, "that could happen."

I wanted to kill him. Why did he say that? Why did he encourage them? "So what if you fight a little? Make up your fights. You can. That's what you're always telling Fred and me."

Mom looked at Dad. "Martin! Don't just sit there! Help me out!"

"It's not my idea," Dad said.

"You agreed!"

"Well, Pat, when you get right down to it, I didn't see that there was anything else I could do."

"Oh!" My mother's face got red. Then she went into this long thing about how she and Dad had problems, but Fred and I didn't have to think about those things, that it was between her and Dad, and they both loved us and that was what counted.

"And, remember, it's just a *trial*," Dad said, "something we're trying out."

"Anyway, first I have to get a job," Mom said.

"I can't move out until I get a job. And, in any case, Ami, you and Fred will stay right here, so that'll be the least disruption for you."

"Why can't you get a job and stay home?" I said. "You could even separate and stay home. I heard about some people who did that. They separated, but they stayed in the same house, because neither one wanted to leave their kids."

"Ami! I don't want to leave you. But I can't stay here, either."

Just a few weeks before they told us, Mom had graduated with an MSW — that's a master's degree in social work. All the time my mother had been in school, Mia's mother would say how great it was that my mom had all that determination, to go back for a degree after twenty years away, and wasn't I proud of her? Yes! I thought we all were. We went to her graduation, and we cheered when the dean handed her the diploma.

Afterward, to celebrate, we ate out in a fancy restaurant that, Dad said, was going to set him back about a month's salary. "I'll pay you back," Mom said. "With interest." I thought it was a joke then.

Right after they told us about the trial separation, Mom started sleeping on the living room couch at night, and typing up résumés and sending them out during the day. She must have sent out a thousand résumés, but she didn't get a job. "Not even a nibble," she said. "Nobody has money to hire. They're laying off people, not hiring."

I was glad. I thought if she didn't get a job, she would change her mind and stay home. And I was glad when Dad said he wanted to "discuss" things with her, and they would go into the kitchen and shut the door, so they could talk in private. But, instead of changing her mind, Mom went right on telling me I had to be more responsible about things like my laundry, because who would do it for me when she was gone? And a lot of times she wouldn't make supper, she wouldn't even be around when we were eating. It was as if she were reallly trying hard to get us all to practice for when she was gone. I'd come home from school sometimes, and the house would be quiet, empty. I'd say to myself, See, Ami, this is how it will feel. It's not so terrible. You can live.

Then the real thing happened. Mom got her job in New Castle and left. And it was terrible. It wasn't like practicing at all. That's why I knew what Ms. Linsley meant about the real thing. Ms. Linsley and I were both sort of in the same boat. She was new at teaching and I was new at living without Mom. One time, when I was in Ms. Linsley's room, she said it was good to have somebody to talk to, and she was glad we were friends.

The thing is, you can't actually be friends with a teacher, not friends like Mia and me. Grown-ups, no matter what they say about being equal, will always remind you who's in charge if they think you're stepping out of line. One afternoon, just a few days before Mia came back to school, I started laughing about something — I forget now what it was — and I couldn't stop. Sometimes laughing is like rain or snow or some other force of nature — it keeps coming and coming, and you can't do anything about it.

That was the way I was laughing. *Whooops! Whooops! Whooops!* Fred says I sound like a whooping crane when I laugh. At first Ms. Linsley laughed with me, then after a few minutes of *whoops! whoops! whoops!* from Ami, she began shaking her head, like, Oh what *is* this!

Which only made me laugh more. She put her chin in her hand and just looked at me. *Whoops! Whooops! Whooops!* Finally, she said, "Okay, Ami, that's enough of preteen hysteria." She didn't say it in a mean way, but I still didn't like it.

Chapter 3

Dad threw something into the shopping cart. "What is it?" I said. It looked like an overgrown tennis ball that had been left out in the rain.

"Celeriac. Didn't we ever have it before?"

"No." I poked it. "Is it alive or dead?"

Dad weighed some tomatoes. "It's just a root veggie, Ami. Ugly, but good." He put his hand on my shoulder. I ducked away. I don't know why. Just recently, it seems I don't want my father always hugging me or putting his arm around me.

I followed him as he strolled through the aisles, looking at different kinds of crackers, tasting the cheese samples, and comparing prices. It takes him forever to do the shopping. We'd already bought everything on our list, but we were still wandering around the market.

"Da-ad." I gave him a significant look and tapped my wristwatch. "School tomorrow." That can usually get him going. He's not the sort of person who lives in the fast lane. Mostly, he ambles along, very relaxed. Which can be helpful or unhelpful, depending on the situation. In my opinion, he had been too relaxed about my mother.

I take it back. That's really unfair. Once my mother made up her mind, I guess there was no way anybody was going to stop her. And Dad tried, he really did. Three or four or five times a week, she and Dad would have what Mom called "the same old arguments, *again*, Martin," and what Dad called "our ongoing discussion." I would hear their voices, Mom's racing, rising and falling, Dad's slow, deep, and deliberate. After a while, she would stop talking, but he wouldn't. Fred says when Dad wants something, he'll wear you down with reasonable "discussions." But he couldn't wear Mom down.

Dad and I walked over to the fish department, and he started sniffing — it was really cute — just like our cat does when the wind is blowing. Our cat's name is Alcott, after Louisa May. Did I say my father is an English teacher? That's why half the things we have are named after dead writers. Our car is Steinbeck (for John Steinbeck) and, if you can believe it, my father's desk is Willie. No, not for William Shakespeare, but some other ancient writer named Maugham, who lived to be about 200 years old. Well, 98 anyway. Or 89, something like that. "Wonderful writer," my father says.

My father looks a lot like Fred. Or should I say Fred looks a lot like Dad? Both of them are sort of medium height and on the skinny side. Fred's better-looking, but my father has a better personality, very gentle and patient. Really, he hardly ever loses his temper. Sometimes kids will come up to me in school and say, "Is Mr. Pelter your father? He's neat!"

At the fish counter, the fish were laid out in ice, their dead eyes staring up at us.

"Fresh cohoe salmon today," the pink man behind the counter said. The fish were gutted open. They were pink, too, outside and inside.

"Let's have that little beauty." Dad pointed to one of the fish.

I couldn't believe it. My father's worst fault is how cheap he is. He's always pointing out to us how much things cost and how little English teachers make. "Dad, it's eight dollars a pound!"

"Fresh cohoe salmon, Ami, you don't see that too often. Think of it as a new experience."

"Maybe I don't want a new experience. What's wrong with tuna fish?"

"We've had it three times a week for the last three months. Tuna fish casserole. Tuna fish sandwiches. Tuna fish loaf. I want something else once in a while, something *I* like."

19

He sounded sort of sad and yet definite, as if he really didn't want me to argue with him. "I just thought, since it's so expensive — "

He took off his glasses and rubbed his eyes. Then a really strange thing happened. Right there in the supermarket, leaning on the fish counter, he started talking to me about Mom. "You know, your mother wanted to get into the world. She never lived on her own, she said she had to find out what it was like."

"I know, Dad." I kicked at the wheels of the cart.

"We were always different. Your mother's much more go go go than I am."

Why did we have to talk about it here?

The man behind the fish counter handed Dad the salmon wrapped in plastic. I thought Dad would take the hint and we'd leave, but he went on talking. "I asked her to go to a marriage counselor; I thought we should all go. You and Fred, too, because I saw it as a family problem. But your mother had other ideas. She said it was no good, it wasn't like patching up a dish that was cracked."

"Don't you think we should get going?" I said. I tugged at the cart. "Do you want some ice cream? Or a frozen pie? Last week you said that frozen strawberry pie was delicious." I was afraid he was going to get himself into a really depressed mood talking about Mom. The first few weeks after she left last summer were ter-

20

rible. Dad hardly talked. We'd sit down to eat supper and he'd pick up his fork and then just sit there. Usually, after a while, Fred or I would say, "You okay, Dad?" And Dad would look up and give this sad, sad smile. It was awful! It made me so mad at my mother. For a long time, I was really furious with her.

"When she first brought up this idea of leaving," Dad went on, "I thought it was just harebrained, some idea she got from a woman's magazine about fulfillment. And then I saw she was serious, I saw that no matter how much I talked and tried to change her mind, she had this one idea that she was getting a job and moving out."

"Dad — "

"She could have held down a job here in Alliance. I wasn't holding her back about that. You know that, don't you? And I told her, any time she wants to come back — "

Suddenly, I thought, Mom is coming back! That's why he's talking this way. To get me ready for it. "She's coming back?" I said. I could hardly breathe. "She's coming back?"

"What?" Dad looked at me blankly for a moment. Then he tossed the package of fish into the cart. "No, honey, no. Oh, no."

When we got home, Fred was in the kitchen, reading the sports page and eating last night's leftovers. "Stop right there," Dad said. "Don't ruin your appetite, Fred. We have something special for supper tonight. Fresh cohoe salmon."

"Fish?" Fred said. He didn't look impressed.

While Dad cooked the salmon, I made french fries and Fred set the table. Alcott hung around, purring and getting between everyone's legs. *He* was certainly enthusiastic about the idea of fish for supper.

When we sat down, Dad put big chunks of salmon on our plates and looked at us expectantly. I took a bite. Soft, and not too much taste. "Mmmm," I said. I didn't want to hurt Dad's feelings.

"So. This is the famous cohoe salmon," Fred said. "Kind of blah, isn't it, Dad? Maybe you didn't cook it right."

"The flavor is subtle, Fred."

"I guess it's wasted on me."

"Could be. Wait until you taste it cold tomorrow, though. That's really special."

"I think I'll pass," Fred said. "I'd rather have cold almost anything than cold fish."

"I don't understand you. This fish is delicious. Where are your taste buds?"

"Well, you have to defend it, Dad. You're the guy who made the mistake of buying the expensive little sucker."

My father's eyebrows shot up.

Silence for a few moments. Then Fred said, "I finally got all the forms filled out for student exchange. Now I wait to hear if I'm in."

"Student exchange?" I said. "When? Where?"

"Where do you think, Ami? France."

When Fred was in sixth grade, he got into an AP conversational French course. Ever since then, he's been a Francophile. Dad's word. It means someone actually in love with everything French. Fred's bedroom is covered with maps and posters of France. He listens to French records and French songs, he gets a monthly French language magazine. Of course, he rides a Peugeot bike, and he's after Dad to buy a Peugeot car. They only cost about twenty thousand dollars!

Fred wants to be a translator, maybe work for the United Nations. I told him that the way he argues with Dad over just about anything, it's a good thing he doesn't want to be a diplomat, someone who has to make peace between people.

"I'll be going in the spring," Fred said. "March, April, May. If I'm lucky, I'll get a family right in Paris."

"You'll be gone for three months?"

"Right. Back in time for exams. Dad, you won't have to think about me for three months. *Voilà!* No arguments for three whole months."

Dad and Fred started talking about the money part of student exchange. I left the table and began washing the dishes. My least favorite house chore, but I couldn't just sit there and listen to Fred sounding so happy about going away. No one had asked me how I felt. Three months was a long time. What guarantee was there that Fred would even come home after those three months? What if he loved France so much he stayed there? It could happen. Mom had been gone five months now and I still wasn't used to it. I didn't think I ever would be. And I wouldn't get used to Fred's being gone for three months next spring, either. When he brought his dishes over to the sink, I said, "Traitor."

"What'd I do now?"

"You know!"

"What? What?"

"France," I muttered, splashing dishes into the water.

Fred looked at me, surprised. "Ami, it's a long way off. Think of it this way. You'll have Dad all to yourself. Anyway, what kind of red-blooded American kid sister are you? I thought you'd be glad to be rid of me."

"You're right! I will be."

"There you go."

"I still think you're a traitor."

Chapter 4

Something fairly embarrassing happened in school. Mia and I were on our way to gym when Ms. Linsley stopped us in the hall. "Ami, hi!" She gave me a big smile. "How are you doing, Ami?"

"Oh. Fine, thanks."

"Hello, Mia. I see you two girls are still tight as two bugs in a rug."

Mia and I laughed politely.

Now here comes the embarrassing part. Ms. Linsley said, "I've invited your father for supper next Friday, Ami. A week from this Friday, that is, and I'd like you and Fred to come, too."

I didn't know what to say. My face got hot. Why would she invite my father to supper?

"Well, you girls better go along or you'll be late."

Mia and I hurried down the hall. "Woo woo," Mia said.

"Shut up, Mia."

"Forrest Lake and your dad."

"Shut up up up, Mia."

"It's *in*teresting, Ami!" She took my arm. "Forrest Lake would be pretty neat as a stepmother."

What a stupid thing to say! We went into the locker room and started changing into our shorts and T-shirts. I slammed my locker door shut.

Mia hung up her skirt. "How come you're breathing so hard?"

I pulled my hair around and began braiding it. "I'm going to cut my hair, I'm going to cut it really short."

"When you get mad at me, you always say you're going to cut your hair."

"Really?" I gave her a cold look. "I mean it this time." I ran up the steps to the gym.

"Ami!" Mia caught me at the top of the stairs. "Why are you so mad? Because of what I said about Forrest Lake? I don't want her to be your stepmother. You know me, old flap mouth, I say everything that comes into my head."

"How many times do I have to tell you, Mia, my parents aren't divorced? They are separated. Which means they are living apart. Which means they could start living together any time. It might

26

be next week or next month, or tomorrow morning!" I pulled open the door. And there, right across the gym, sitting in the top bleacher, was Robert Volz.

Mia saw Robert at the same moment I did. "It's him. Ami, it's him."

"I know." There were other kids there, too. The study halls are always overflowing, so every period the monitor picks five or six kids to take their books into the gym.

"I can't bear it," Mia whispered. "He's so adorable. He looks just like a tweetie bird, the way his hair sticks up in those funny little tufts."

"Redheaded tweetie bird," I said.

Mia snickered. "Amikins," she said and squeezed my hand.

After a moment, I squeezed back and said, "Miaseea."

That's the way we almost always make up. I know the names are sort of childish, but we started it way back when we first became friends and we still do it.

"Okay, gals and guys, let's go!" Mr. Cooper stood in the middle of the gym, his hands on his hips, and led us through warm-ups. Mr. Cooper always wears white shorts, a white shirt, white socks, and a white sweatband. He's blond and extremely handsome. A lot of the girls have crushes on him. "Why didn't Ms. Linsley pick on him for supper?" I whispered to Mia.

Robert stayed in the gym the whole period.

27

Once, when I looked at him, he was bent over, his chin in his hand, reading one of his books. Another time he was talking to Alex Takamura. But a couple of times, when I glanced up, I was almost positive he was looking over my way. Well, half positive. It seemed more like he was watching Mia.

After warm-ups, we played basketball. Mr. Cooper divided us into teams and handed out colored armbands. He put Mia and me on opposing teams. He always does. Some teachers are like that; as soon as they know Mia and I are friends, they separate us.

Mr. Cooper always makes us take a team name. "It improves team spirit, people! And you can't win a game without team spirit. Okay, you boys and girls over there, purple armbands, what's your team name?" He snapped his fingers and we all started shouting out names. "Just one of you!" Mr. Cooper yelled. "You, Ami, give me a name."

I bet he chose me because of my voice — I mean that he heard it over the other kids. It was embarrassing. "The Purple People?" I said. Everybody on my team groaned.

"The Purple People it is," Mr. Cooper yelled. "Okay, orange bands, gimme a name." They chose Orange Juicers.

I'm pretty good at basketball; usually I make about five baskets for my team. It helps that I'm tall. "Dunk it, Ami!" Bunny Larrabee shouted.

She's the next tallest girl in our class. I can't actually dunk the ball — I'm not that tall and I'm not Jabbar — but it's fun to dribble down the floor and shoot, leaping into the air. I only made three baskets, though. I was sort of flustered because of Robert. Mia didn't make any baskets for the Orange Juicers — no surprise, she loathes basketball or any sport — but the Orange Juicers won, anyway, because Bruno Morelli (the boy we used to love in fourth grade) is a superstar player. Alex Takamura and a couple of the other boys went "Yaaay!" every time Bruno made a basket. Robert just sat there and watched.

Chapter 5

"Do you think he knows we're following him?" Mia said.

"I hope not."

We walked up and down the street with our arms linked, looking into store windows. It was drizzling, but we were pretending to window-shop. What we were really doing was waiting for Robert Volz to come out of McDonald's across the street. We had followed him and two other boys, Miles Haymond and Alex Takamura, downtown after school.

"Well, do you think he saw us?"

"I didn't think so."

"I hope not!" she said. "Oh, I forgot to tell you, Ami. Wait till you hear! Last night, I went over to the mall, shopping with my mom. And I saw him!"

"Robert?"

"Do you know any other *him*? He and Miles were in the record store, right up in front. You know, where they have the marked-down records? Two seconds after I see him, my mother says, 'Oh, let's go in there, I promised Stacey a record for improving her math marks.' Ami, I almost died! We would have had to walk right by Robert and Miles, and you know my mother. She would have made me introduce her. I literally dragged her away by the arm."

I thought about Mia shopping with her mom and I started feeling sad. Not that I ever shopped that much with my mother, but it was the idea. Mia could shop with her mother any time she wanted to. "You didn't tell me you saw Robert. You know we're supposed to tell each other everything. This whole day passed and you didn't tell me."

"Well, I'm telling you now," Mia said.

"Thanks a lot. Next time you can wait a week to tell me the news."

"Ooooh, Ami. Are you getting mad at me again?"

"No."

"Yes, you are."

"No, I'm not."

"Yes, you are."

"No, I'm not."

31

"Yes you are, yes you are, yes you are." The rain made her face shine.

I know Mia, she would have gone on like that forever. "You're right, I'm mad mad mad at you."

We both started laughing. Our perverted sense of humor. Then I felt better and, right away, I got the most awful hunger pangs. When I feel good, I always want to eat. Then, to make it worse, Mia said, "I wonder what Robert's eating."

I looked across the street. "Hamburgers. Big, juicy hamburgers. And lots of fries. With ketchup and mustard." My stomach rumbled. "I'm starved. Let's go in there and get something to eat, too."

Mia put her hand on her heart. "What if he sees us?"

"Mia, come on! We see Robert every day in school."

"That's different. We can't help that."

"Okay, we won't look at him, Mia. We'll turn our backs. We'll just sit down, like we don't even know he and Miles and Alex are there."

"Wait, let's just wait a little longer. Are you okay, Ami? Can you hold out?" She dug in her pocketbook. "Look, here's a chocolate mint I saved just for — Ami! They're coming out! There they are!" We held hands and breathed hard.

The boys stood on the corner, talking.

"So close," Mia said. "Rob-ert. Oh, Rob-ert.

32

Don't you think he's the cutest one, Ami?"

"We have to be loyal to Robert, but Alex is fairly adorable." He had black hair and looked just like Matt Dillon.

"But Robert is so lovable. That red hair. I die."

"I like his glasses. They make him look sweet."

"You're right. I just love our redheaded tweetie bird, Robert. Those little tufts of hair!"

"Alex is so good-looking. I bet he's conceited," I said.

"What about Miles?" Mia said. "He has a nice face, but he's fat."

"I don't think he's that fat. You think his face is nice? He's always scowling. He just had a nice juicy hamburger, and he's still scowling."

I pulled up my slicker hood. The rain was coming down harder. The boys started walking and window-shopping across the street. On our side, we stopped when they stopped, we looked in the store windows and watched them out of the corner of our eyes. After a few minutes they went into a peanut store and came out cracking peanuts.

"Hamburgers," I said sadly. "Fries. Sodas. Peanuts."

Next, they went into a drugstore. We hung around a shoe store, listening to my stomach rumble.

"Don't think about food," Mia said. "It only makes it worse."

33

"I'm not thinking about food, Mia, my *stomach's* thinking about it. You know what they're doing in there? Stuffing their faces. I bet they're eating Eskimo Pies right now. I bet they've got their pockets full of chocolate bars."

"Poor Ami! Am I really making you suffer?"

Just then the boys came out of the drugstore and started across the street, straight toward us.

Mia grabbed my arm. "What should we do?"

"What can we do? Say hello."

"I can't breathe! I'm having a heart attack!"

"I'll come and visit you in the hospital."

At the last moment, just before we would have had to speak to them, the three boys turned in the other direction and walked away. Mia and I stared after them.

"I have this horrible feeling," Mia said.

"Me, too."

"Are you thinking what I'm thinking?"

"I'm afraid I am."

"Are you thinking they knew we were following them?"

"I'm afraid I am."

"Oh, Ami. They know! I just want to die."

"Me, too," I said. "But first, can I have something to eat?"

Chapter 6

Friday morning, when I came down to breakfast, the first thing I saw was a little chipmunk Alcott had killed and left on the rug by the door. I don't understand why Alcott has to kill chipmunks when we feed him twice a day. I picked up the tiny corpse and tossed it into the bushes. It made me feel really bad, and the whole day seemed to go wrong from that moment on.

To begin with, Dad and Fred almost had a fight at the breakfast table. It started when Fred said he wouldn't be eating supper at Ms. Linsley's that night with us. "I have other plans. Jan and I are going to a movie."

Dad broke eggs into a bowl. "Invite Jan for supper, too, Fred — Ami, make us some toast —

35

I'll clear it with Forrest, Fred. I'm sure it'll be okay with her."

"No, thanks." Fred opened his French book and started reading with a definite *discussion over* look on his face.

"Is it a matter of not enough time, Fred?" Dad turned the flame up on the stove. "What time does the movie start?"

"Dad, it doesn't make any difference if I go to supper there or not. So, why go?"

"Well, I think it does make a difference." Dad put the eggs on the table and sat down. "Fred, I'd like to have you there and so would Forrest."

"She's not interested in me," Fred said. "That's a purely political invitation."

"Political invitation?" I said. "What does that mean? What are you talking about?"

"Ms. Linsley's running for office. Four-letter title beginning with *w*. Rhymes with *strife*."

"Wait one second!" Dad said. "Slow down, Fred. Forrest and I are just friends. Further-more — " Dad glanced at me.

I picked up my fork and waited. *Futhermore, your mother is coming back home to live. The trial period is over. It didn't work.*

" — furthermore," Dad said, "Forrest is a fine person and I don't want to hurt her feelings."

"But I still don't want to come," Fred said. He pushed back his chair. "I'm not her friend. Okay? Can we leave it at that?"

"No, we can't leave it at that. You were in-

36

vited. I want you to come. I don't think your reason for not coming is sufficient."

"Are you ordering me?"

"Fred, when do I order you to do things? I would like you to show up at Forrest's home for supper, but of your own free will."

"Then of my own free will, I'll pass this time."

They kept looking at each other. Their faces are so much alike! But Dad's face gets almost white when he's mad, while Fred's face flushes. Finally, Dad shrugged. "Suit yourself, Fred." And he turned to me. "I can count on you, can't I, Ami?"

I felt right in the middle, but I said, "Sure, Dad." What I really wanted to say was the same thing Fred had said. *I'll pass.* And more, too. *You're still married to Mom, I don't think you should be having dates.* I thought it, but I couldn't get it out.

When I met Mia on the way to school, she said, "Ami! I have something to tell you!" She put her arm around my waist. "First, I have a question for you. Don't rush your answer. This is a biggie. What color are Robert's eyes?"

It was hard for me to stop thinking about Ms. Linsley and Dad. "Blue," I said.

"Wrong! That's what I thought, too. But they're brown! I saw him with his glasses off in Mrs. Giordono's office."

"When? You didn't tell me you saw him, Mia." Suddenly, I got upset all over again. "Why do I have to keep saying this to you? We're supposed to tell each other *everything*."

Mia dropped her arm from around my waist. "I know, I know. Don't yell at me. I just forgot until this moment. Anyway, it was only the other day. Remember when I was late meeting you? I walked into the office to get a late pass. And there he was, for the same thing. He was late, too!"

"You were both late?"

"Yes! Isn't that amazing?"

"Did he say anything?"

"No. But he had his glasses off and he looked right at me. His eyes are definitely brown."

Later, for some reason, that conversation kept going around in my head. *His eyes are definitely brown.* World-shaking news, Mia. What if I'd said that to her, in just that mean, sarcastic way? But I never would. It was just like the morning — I didn't want to hurt Dad's feelings. I didn't want to hurt Mia's feelings. But was that the true reason I didn't say it? Or was it because I was too much of a coward to tell people what I really thought?

Mia came home with me after school. We made sandwiches and milk shakes and took them up to my room. After we ate, we took the archives box down from my closet. Mia still gags every time she sees Raymond Fuller's bubble gum. "Just don't look at it," I said.

"I can't help it. Don't you ever have a feeling

38

like you *have* to look at something, or think about something, and you *definitely* don't want to, but you do it, anyway?''

I got out the notebook. I knew what she meant. It was like thinking about my mother.

I opened the notebook and passed it to Mia. "You start."

Across the top of a sheet of paper, Mia wrote, SEEING ROBERT IN THE OFFICE. Then on the next line, *It was an unexpected thrill. I walked in and there he was, leaning coolly against the counter. I would have recognized that flaming red hair anywhere!* Mia is really good at writing our reports. If it were up to me, I would probably write something like, "We saw him. He was wearing his Prince T-shirt. We thought he looked cute." But Mia makes everything sound better.

To my utter surprise, she continued, *his eyes were not sky blue, but a deep, sad brown, like the color of autumn leaves.* She bit the pen. "Anything else about his eyes?''

"I think we used deep, sad brown for Bruno.''

"How can you remember that far back?''

"Well, you always write stuff like deep, sad brown.''

"I do? That's terrible! Uggh! I'll never use those words again!'' She chewed on the pen. "We need something different, but now all I can think of is deep, sad brown; deep, sad brown. You're right, Ami, I'm in a rut.'' She crossed out the end of her sentence and pushed the notebook over to me. "You write something about his eyes."

The only thing I could think of was the chipmunk Alcott had killed. "What about — eyes the color of chipmunk fur?"

"That's not very romantic. Okay, okay, let me write something else."

I didn't like the way she grabbed the notebook back. "Give me a chance, Mia. You can't make up the whole thing."

"I'm not making it up, Ami. It happened to me. I walked in the office and I saw Robert, and he took off his glasses, and I saw — "

"I know. I know! I've heard it now a dozen times. What I mean is, even when it happens to one of us, it's supposed to be like it happened to both of us. You know that's the way we do things. And that's why you should have told me right away."

"I *said* I was sorry! Do you want me to go home?"

I almost said yes. I didn't understand why we were fighting. I didn't understand anything. Why did I feel so awful? Because Alcott killed a chipmunk? Because Mia saw Robert without me? Because I was eating supper at Ms. Linsley's house?

I looked out the window, at our street and all the houses, one next to the other. Mrs. Demoley was wheeling her baby twins. Vance Carley was making a huge racket on his motorbike. Nothing felt real. It was like seeing things in a movie.

I leaned my forehead against the glass. A plum tree grows right outside my window. It has a shaggy black trunk and every summer it produces tiny sour plums that no one likes. "Every morning when I wake up, I see the branches of that tree," I said.

"I know," Mia said.

"We've lived in this house for six years."

"I know."

"The plum tree's grown a lot since we moved here. I wonder how old it is." Suddenly, I thought about the tree dying, no white flowers in spring, no red plums in summer. "What if it dies? What if somebody chops it down?"

"Who's going to do that?"

"I don't know! All sorts of crazy things happen. It could happen while I was in school. Somebody could just come along with an ax. What if I wake up tomorrow and the tree is gone?"

"It won't be," Mia said.

"How do you know?"

"Ami! The plum tree will be there tomorrow morning."

I shrugged. "Maybe."

"Maybe!" Mia clapped her hands to her head. "I've got a crazy friend, folks! She thinks a fifteen-foot plum tree is going to disappear overnight! Ami, take my word for it, little plum tree is safe. Nobody is going to harm little plum tree. Look." She showed me what she had written in the notebook. . . . *eyes the color of chipmunk fur.*

"Take it out," I said, "it's awful."

"I like it."

"It was better the way you had it."

"I'm serious, Ami, it's really better your way. I've got to stop writing things like autumn leaves. Autumn leaves! That's so boring. If I gave your father my paper, I bet he'd write CLICHÉ all over it!"

"Well," I said, "if he doesn't like autumn leaves, how come he likes Forrest?" It was such a crazy thing to say, we both started laughing.

Chapter 7

"Ami, what's the cross street?" Dad peered out
the car window. He's really nearsighted.

"Willow Road."

"We're looking for Danvers."

"I know." I touched the little pearl studs in
my ears. Mom had given them to me for my
twelfth birthday. Maybe we wouldn't be able to
find the street where Ms. Linsley lived. We'd
drive right by without seeing it. By the time we
realized our mistake, it would be too late to go
over there.

Just as I was thinking that, the engine started
huffing and choking. "What's going on?" Dad
rapped on the dashboard with his knuckles.

I held on to the seat. The engine sounded like
it wasn't long for this world. For a moment I

was hopeful. I saw the whole thing — Steinbeck breaking down. The tow truck. Too late to go to Ms. Linsley's. Dad would call her and — no, even better, he'd forget to call. Then Ms. Linsley would get mad, tell him he was thoughtless and had ruined her dinner. Next, a big fight. And that would be that. The quick end of a short friendship.

Steinbeck bucked again. "White gas," I said. "The last time, all it needed was a can of carburetor cleaner."

"Probably right," Dad said. He pulled into a gas station. I poured the white gas into the tank while he went inside to check our directions. Danvers was just around the corner, a long, steep hill with houses way up above street level on both sides.

Once, when I was really little, I was walking up a hill with my mother and I started to cry, because I was sure we were both going to fall off the top and get smashed. She picked me up and carried me. I remembered how she smelled, like cold air and tangerines.

"Dad?" I said. "Dad, don't — " I didn't know how to say what I felt. I pressed my head against the car window.

He looked over at me. "Ami, are you okay? What's the matter, honey? What is it?"

"I don't think we should go there," I said to the window. "You're still married to Mom. Can't you make up? Let her come home. Talk about your problems."

"Ami, I'm not keeping Pat from coming back."

The way he said *Pat* — "If she came home tomorrow, would you be glad?"

He didn't answer right away. Finally, he said, "Truthfully? I don't know, honey. It's just not that simple, anymore. . . ." That's when I noticed he wasn't wearing his wedding ring.

After that, it didn't seem like there was anything else to say.

Ms. Linsley lived in a tall old building at the very end of the street. We went up a steep flight of crumbling cement steps. "Hello, Pelter people." She was waiting at the top of the steps. "Don't you look nice, Ami. And you, Martin!"

She put her hand on Dad's arm. She was wearing jeans, little blue ballet slippers, and a white blouse with a cat embroidered on each sleeve. "Isn't that neat, Ami? My mother made it for me. She knows I love cats. You do, too, don't you?" She held the door open. "Ami, by the way, call me Forrest, please. We're not in school now."

I walked by her into the room. There were three cats sitting on a window seat. One was all gray, one was black with white ears, and one was white with orange spots. I started toward them; then I saw that there was somebody else in the room, too, a boy with short, curly hair and really big ears.

"Ami, this is Jones," Ms. Linsley said. "My nephew. You two should like each other."

"Hi," Jones said, looking bored.

"Hi." I went over to pet the cats. Did she invite Jones for me? So she could concentrate on Dad?

We sat down at the table and Ms. Linsley poured wine for her and Dad, and soda for me and her nephew. "Let's see, have we got anything to toast? Martin?"

"Hmm." Dad put his chin in his hand and thought. "Okay." He raised his glass, then waited until we all raised our glasses. "I propose a toast to friendship and friends, without which a difficult world would be a much more difficult and unkind place."

"Oh, how nice!" Ms. Linsley clinked her glass against Dad's, then I had to clink my glass against Jones's, and we all drank to Dad's toast. I liked his toast, too. I thought of Mia, and it seemed really true. But I didn't like the way Ms. Linsley kept giving him glowing looks while they sipped the wine.

I was thirsty and drank the soda too fast. What was I going to talk about to Jones?

Ms. Linsley and Dad didn't have any trouble talking. First they talked about school, then about cars, then about hiking in the Adirondacks. She talked fast and laughed a lot. Dad laughed a lot, too — more, in fact, than I'd seen him laugh in ages.

"I go to JVS Middle," Jones said to me.

"Oh."

"Where do you go?"

"Drumlins Middle."

46

"Your name is Ami?"

I nodded.

"I'm in eighth grade."

"Seventh."

"You have nice hair. I always see at least one nice thing in every girl. Last year, my class voted me Biggest Flirt."

"Really." I looked over at the cats. They were still in the same place. Maybe Ms. Linsley fed them before we came, so they'd be well behaved and make a good impression on us. I wished I could go sit with them.

"More steak à l'Allemande, Ami?" Ms. Linsley said.

"No, thank you." It was really just hamburger with a fancy name.

"How is my steak à l'Allemande, folks?"

"Well — " Dad began.

"No, Martin, I can't trust you. You're too sweet and tactful. I'm asking Jones. He'll tell me the truth, won't you, Jones?" She was talking to Jones, but laughing and glancing at my father. "Jones always tells the truth, don't you, Jones?"

"Except when I'm lying." He looked at me. "Do you think I'm lying or telling the truth when I say that?"

I hate riddles like that. Maybe he thought I was dumb because I hadn't said anything.

Dessert was strawberry shortcake. Usually that's my favorite dessert. Ms. Linsley cut big triangular slices for everyone. "It looks luscious,

47

doesn't it?" she said. Jones scooped up a big spoonful of cream and shoved it in his mouth. Everybody was chewing and swallowing.

"We had a class newspaper last year, sort of like a yearbook," Jones said. "Everyone who got voted something got their picture in it. You know what my picture said? Biggest Flirt."

"You told me."

"I made a mistake. I was really voted Most Handsome."

Ms. Linsley looked over, "Ami, he's putting you on."

She didn't have to tell me that.

Dad reached across Ms. Linsley for the coffee-pot. His arm brushed against her arm. All of a sudden, I just couldn't sit there any longer. I got up and left. I knew they all thought I was going to the bathroom, but instead I went out the door. "Ami?" Dad called. "Where're you going?"

"I'll be right back." I think I said it. Maybe I didn't. I ran down the stairs.

And then outside, I ran straight down the hill, as if somebody were pushing me. I could almost feel a hand at my back. *Go! Go!* I didn't know where I was going, I just had to run. At the bottom of the hill, I stopped to shake a pebble out of my sneaker, and saw a telephone booth on the corner. I went in and called Mia.

"This is Ami, Mrs. Jenson."

"Oh, okay, dear, hang on, Mia's right here."

"Ami?" Mia said, "I thought you were at Forrest Lake's house."

"I am. I mean, I'm not. I'm in a phone booth. I couldn't stand it another second. You know what she said to us? Hello, Pelter people. Pelter people! I bet she thought that was adorable."

"What'd your father say?"

"He likes everything she says. Then she said to me, 'Ami, call me Forrest.' "

"Did you?"

"No. I wouldn't." On the wall of a market across the street, someone had spray painted in big red letters, I'M SERIOUSLY SEARCHING. My eyes kept going back to it. Seaching for what? Searching where? What was *serious* searching?

"She has three cats," I said.

"So she can't be aaaall bad," Mia said.

"Her nephew is there. He goes to JVS. Eighth grade."

"Is he cute?"

"He's got big ears."

"You-know-who has big ears, too."

"This guy's ears are much bigger and so is his ego. You know what he said? Last year when he was in seventh grade, they voted him Biggest Flirt. I wish you were here, Mia."

"I'll come right over."

"Come on, then."

"Wouldn't that be something? I'd say, 'Hi, you all, I just got lonely for Ami.' " She lowered her voice. "I looked up you-know-who's phone number. And you'll never believe this. It's incredible, but his number is six-six-three, six-three-nine-three."

I knew she wanted me to say something. "We never had one with so many threes in it."

"I know! This is a first, Ami. It has to mean something special. Maybe we should call him three times right away. We could do it the first day we call him. Or maybe three times the first week. We have to figure this out."

We talked a while more, then I went back to Ms. Linsley's.

They all looked up when I walked in. Dad was sitting on the couch with one leg stretched out in front of him. There was a pan of ice on the floor, and Ms. Linsley was kneeling in front of him, wrapping an Ace bandage around his ankle.

"Ami," Dad said, half rising, then sitting down fast. "Where were you?"

"What happened?"

Dad grimaced. "I started to go after you and tripped and — "

"He fell down the stairs," Jones said.

"Not all the stairs," Ms. Linsley said quickly. "Just four or five."

"More like forty or fifty," Dad said. "What a klutz."

"No, Martin, it's those awful steep steps. I think you should sue my landlord." Ms. Linsley finished wrapping Dad's ankle with tape. "Anyway, my Red Cross training finally paid off. Ice a sprain, decrease the pain." She picked up the pan of ice and went into the kitchen.

50

"Does it hurt?" I said.

"It did. It's not too bad now. So where were you?"

"Yeah, Ami, where were you?" Jones said.

I sat down on the couch next to Dad and stared at his bandaged ankle. "I just — I went out for a walk. I'm sorry, Dad."

Ms. Linsley came back. "Martin? Think you can make it into the kitchen and keep me company while I clean up the dishes?"

"Sure thing." Dad limped into the kitchen, leaning on her, his hand on her shoulder, right next to her neck.

Jones turned on the TV. "That was cute the way you ran out."

I could hear Dad and Ms. Linsley talking in the kitchen.

"Real cute little attention-getter. Do you do things like that a lot?"

"All the time," I said. I reached past him and turned up the sound on the TV.

Chapter 8

A couple of days later, Mia and I were babysitting for her little sister, Sara. The baby was sleeping when Mia's mother went out. "She ought to wake up in about ten minutes," Mrs. Jenson said, but Sara just went on sleeping. We hung out in Mia's room, doing makeup and checking Sara every few minutes. She kept sleeping.

"Isn't she cute the way she sleeps?" Mia said. Sara had her fist jammed in her mouth and her little butt pushed up in the air. We went back to Mia's room. "Your mother shouldn't pay me. I'm not doing anything."

"Just wait until Sara wakes up. She makes you run your buns off doing stuff for her. You know what we could do while we're waiting?" Mia painted on a streak of midnight-blue eyeshadow. "We could call you-know-who."

"Want to?" I curled my lashes with mascara.

"I do, if you do." She looked at me in the mirror. "You've got mascara all over the place. Should we do it the way we did last year?"

"You mean, say, 'Is this Robert?' and then — "

"Uh-huh." Mia handed me a tissue. "We're so goofy!"

We both laughed. We went in to check Sara again. Still sleeping. It's incredible how much babies can sleep. Then we went across the hall into Mia's parents' bedroom and sat down on the bed. They have a red push-button phone. Mia punched in Robert's number and held the receiver out to me.

I shook my head. "You first."

She rolled her eyes and held the phone to her ear. I could hear it ringing in Robert's house. Suddenly, Mia hung up. "Oh, my heart! It's beating so hard!" She fell over on the bed. "I almost died doing that. Ami! You almost lost your best friend." She sat up. "I can see the headline. LOVESICK GIRL DIES DIALING DARLING BOY'S NUMBER!"

We checked Sara once more. "Should we call him again?" I whispered over the crib. Mia took a deep breath and nodded.

This time I punched the number.

Mia held the receiver to her ear. "Ami! Quick!

What'll I say? Tell me something to say, Ami. I just forgot everything. I'm blank! I've lost my memory."

We were both laughing so hard we could hardly speak. "You say hello. And then — and then you say, 'Is Robert there?' "

The phone rang. "Yes. Yes. Then what?"

"And then when he comes on — don't you remember this? You say, 'Robert?' And he says, 'Yes.' And you say, 'Is this Robert Smith?' "

Mia stared at me, her hand over her mouth. "Okay, and — ?"

"And he says, 'No, this is Robert Volz.' And you say, 'Oh, excuse me, I must have the wrong number.' "

"I admire you," she whispered. "You don't lose your head!"

The phone rang and rang. Then Sara started crying, so we hung up and went in to her. She was kicking her arms and legs, like a tiny windmill.

Mia reached into the crib. "I better change this kid. She's soaked to the eyeballs."

I got a diaper out of the box. "You want me to do it?"

"No." She pulled off Sara's wet diaper.

One thing I don't like about baby-sitting Sara is that Mia is really exclusive with her. Mrs. Jenson hires us both, but Mia hardly ever lets me carry Sara or give her a bottle or do anything for her.

"I saw your father using a cane today in school," Mia said. She powdered Sara's bottom.

"It takes the weight off his ankle." At lunchtime, I'd seen Dad limp into the cafeteria with Ms. Linsley. Dad was listening to something she was telling him, leaning in toward her, nodding and smiling. Everything about her was in motion — her mouth, her eyes, her hands flying up and out. A giant windmill.

I put my big finger into Sara's small fat hand. "You are so funny-looking." Sara grinned, and spit went down the side of her mouth. "Oooh, you like my hand. Don't eat it, funny-looking babby."

"Don't call her funny-looking," Mia said. "She can hear you!"

"Mia, she doesn't know those words."

"Babies aren't dumb, Ami. They understand tons more than you think. Anyway, she's beautiful."

"Oh, the funny-looking babby." I don't know why I said it again. To tease Mia, maybe. Or to get my mind off Dad and Ms. Linsley. "Fat, funny-looking babby. Yes, you are funny-looking, funny, funny-looking!"

Mia frowned and pulled up the crib bars. "Your father looks like a war hero with that cane," she said. "I bet Ms. Linsley thinks so, too. Woo woo!"

"Mia, do you have to say that?"

"What? War hero?"

"*Woo woo.* You're always saying that."

"I do not always say that." She gave Sara a yellow plastic ring to play with.

"You say it lots of times, and it's really dumb."

"When? When did I say it before?"

"Mia, you say it so many times, you don't even hear yourself saying it anymore."

"What's so terrible about woo woo, anyway?"

"I told you, it's irritating and *dumb.*"

"Woo woo!" she woo wooed into my face. I felt really angry. I pushed her away. In fact, I shoved her pretty hard. She flipped her braids over her shoulder. "What's your problem, Ami?"

"You," I said. We went downstairs, into the kitchen. Mia got out crackers and jam and poured herself a glass of milk. She sat down and made a whole bunch of cracker and jam sandwiches and started eating them. She didn't ask me if I wanted anything.

I sat down, too, and ate some crackers. I could have taken milk and jam if I wanted it. Mia's mother always says, "Ami, don't be a guest in this house. Make yourself at home."

I didn't feel very hungry, but I kept eating crackers anyway. Mia poured some more milk. Neither of us said anything. I picked up a rubber baby ball from the floor and bounced it. "A, my name is Ami, and I'm allergic to all artichokes. I'm also an animal for apples and apricots and in the afternoon — "

Mia didn't crack a smile. "No use throwing

56

pearls before swine," I said. Which is what my
father says when Fred or I don't get one of his
jokes or stories. That didn't amuse Mia, either.
She went outside and got the newspaper. She
spread it open on the table and started reading.

I stood up. "I'm going home."

"Wait a sec," Mia said. "You have to hear this.
My horoscope. This is really incredible. 'Someone
you admire,' " she read, " 'will ask you to take
on a difficult task. Don't panic. You can do it.'
Someone you admire. What did I say to you
upstairs?"

"Woo woo."

"No, bozo! Before, when we were calling el-
Roberto. I said. 'You are someone I admire.' Isn't
that an unbelievable coincidence? I just said it
and now it's here, in my horoscope."

"And I already asked you to take on a difficult
task."

"You did?"

"Yes. Not to say woo woo!"

"Oh! Right." She smiled and pulled her chair
over next to mine. "Want a sip of my milk?"

"Sorry I pushed you," I said.

"No, I was being stupid."

"Well, I shouldn't have called Sara funny-
looking. You're right, anyway. She's beautiful."

"Don't worry, I'll never say woo woo again."

"I don't actually care that much."

"Well, I won't, anyway. Let's kiss and make
up!"

We kissed on both cheeks, first one, then the

other. "That's the way the French do it," I said.

"According to fabulous Fred, the famous French expert, I suppose."

"Who else?"

Just then, when we were still kissing, Mia's sister Stacey came in from outside. Stacey is two years older than we are. She doesn't look or act anything like Mia. She's this very thin, sarcastic person. She was wearing sweats and running sneakers and had her hair shoved up on top of her head with one of those red plastic clothespin clips. "Oh, gawd," she said, "the lovebirds."

"Hello, Stacey," Mia said. "Where were you, running?"

Stacey stuck her mouth under the faucet and took a long drink of cold water. "Brilliant deduction, Doctor Watson."

"Looks like you had a good run," Mia said, still trying to be nice.

"Give the little lady sixty-four dollars!" Stacey stuck her finger in the peanut butter jar and licked off a big glob of peanut butter.

"Do you want a spoon?" Mia said.

"Huh?" Stacey said, acting dumb.

"Do you have to eat that way?"

"Yeah yeah yeah, I do."

"I thought you were supposed to be mature."

"Yeah yeah yeah." She ate some more peanut butter.

"I'm never eating that peanut butter again."

Stacey licked her fingers. "You're breaking my heart."

Mia and I went upstairs to check on Sara again. "You're lucky you have Fred for a brother," Mia said.

"He's all right."

"He's civilized, at least."

We tiptoed into Sara's room. She was lying on her back, cooing up at the ceiling. I thought about next spring, March, April, and May, when Fred would be gone. Dad and I would be the only ones left in our house. Just two out of four. In Mia's house, there'd still be five people, her whole family, just like there was now.

Chapter 9

Saturday morning, Fred and Jan drove me to the bus station. I'm always sort of nervous on the weekends that I go to visit my mother. I mean, before I go, I'm nervous. Once I'm there, it's different. I don't know why I get so nervous. It's the same way I feel when I have to take an exam. I don't like to talk much, and I start chewing on the ends of my hair. When my mother was home, she was always trying to break me of the habit. She'd say, "Ami, honey, if you only knew — it makes your hair smell like a wet dog."

As soon as I got in the backseat of the car, I noticed that my hair was wet and smelly. I must have been chewing it at breakfast.

"Sit closer," Fred said to Jan. She scooted over

a little on the front seat. "Closer," he said.

"That's close enough."

"Not for me."

"Well, it is for me, frogface."

Jan is a math wizard, maybe even a genius, but you'd never know it from just talking to her. Fred says she's the real stuff. She and Fred have been going together for almost a year, ever since Jan moved here from someplace called Roscoe, Illinois. It's the longest Fred's ever gone with a girl. When I told Jan that, she said, "Me, too, Ami. I've never gone with a guy for more than two months." So I have this idea that they might get married. I'd really like that, although it wouldn't be until they've both gone to college. Fred says Jan is going to walk off with all the math prizes and scholarships when she graduates.

"So how're things in the seventh grade, Ami?" she said.

"Okay."

"Anything bizarre, crazy, or foolish happen lately?"

Jan asks that every time she sees me. I finally figured out what to say. "So much, that I couldn't tell you all of it."

Jan laughed. "Did I ever tell you about the mathdown I was in, in junior high?"

I leaned over the backseat. "What's a mathdown?" Then I leaned back in case she could smell my hair.

"You know, like a spelling bee, only for math. Three of us went to meet a math team from Roosevelt, our most hated rival school. Me, Donny Evvert, and Lisa Skolnick," she said. "We were the little shining lights of the junior high math department. Everybody said we were going to cream the other team. We were so sure of ourselves! We were going to wing it, but our advisor said, 'You kids want to go to meet Roosevelt, you kids prepare.' So we moaned and groaned, but we prepared. Then! When we got to Roosevelt that day, we were in our usual jeans and shirts. *Their* team came out all dressed up. In black. Total black. Like they were going to a funeral. Guess what, they were. Ours. They whipped us so bad, we just slunk out of there."

"How come that didn't teach you a little humility?" Fred said. "You could use it."

"Look who's talking. The French chef, himself."

"How'd you do in the French test, by the way?"

"Don't mention it. How'd you do?"

"What do you think? Aced it."

"Ratface! I just made it through."

"Come to France," Fred said. Now he sounded serious. "That's the way to really learn French. You've still got time to apply."

Jan turned around again. "Do you believe this guy, Ami? Your loony tunes brother — "

"What's so loony about it?" Fred said.

"You want me to live your life, Fred?" Jan

sounded serious, too. "This isn't the dark ages, you know."

I had the feeling they'd talked about this a whole lot of times before. They were edgy with each other. I scrunched back in my seat. I don't like being around people when they're fighting. It's sort of like eavesdropping, only worse when it's your own family.

"France is for you," Jan said, "and math is for me. I can't afford to lose three months."

"You know it all already."

"Oh, how can you say that! Fred, that's stupid! Do you know everything about France?"

"Look, don't call me stupid."

Jan moved all the other way over to the window. Neither of them said anything. Did everybody fight? Didn't it mean anything when you loved someone? Wasn't that enough? Maybe they were going to break up; that was the way it started with my parents. Nobody said anything to anybody until Fred pulled up in front of the bus station. I put on my knapsack. "Thanks for the ride."

"Tell Mom I'll drive down to see her. Maybe next weekend."

"Okay. Bye. Bye, Jan." I got out.

"Ami?" I turned around. Jan had her head out the window. "Have a good time!" She threw me a kiss, which was nice, but I would have felt a whole lot better if she and Fred hadn't had that fight.

The bus trip to New Castle takes almost three

hours. I had a lunch with me and a paperback book. The last time I went down to visit my mother, a woman in a red blouse sat next to me. She put her head back and closed her eyes. "Don't talk to me," she said. I wasn't even going to.

I sat down and this time a boy in blue jeans took the seat next to me. I was feeling sort of upset because of Jan and Fred, and I decided if the boy in blue jeans told me not to talk, I'd tell him to go find himself another seat.

"Good morning, ladies and gentlemen," the bus driver said. "May I have your attention, please. Smoking only in the rear. Cigarettes only, please, no cigars, no pipes, and no wacky weeds. Thank you and have a pleasant trip."

The bus started. The boy opened a magazine and put on a pair of horn-rimmed glasses. That's when I realized he wasn't a boy at all, but a man — the tiniest grown man I'd ever seen. A miniman.

He wore shiny, polished moccasins. Each little foot was about half the size of one of my sneakers. He pushed his glasses up on his little nose, coughed, and patted his mouth with his little hand. He acted just like anybody normal, but then I had this strange thought. What if he came from outer space? What if he was a representative of some other species? A tiny, very smart species come to find out about us giants, who were doing so many dumb things on earth. All of a sudden he put down his magazine and said, "Where are you going?"

I jumped. "N-New Castle."

"New Castle. Nice town. They hear me. Right on the edge of my territory."

My skin prickled. *Hear me? Territory?* Was I right? Were there other tiny aliens? A whole band of little peoplelike beings, all with their own territories?

"Since we're seatmates," he said, "we might as well introduce ourselves."

I thought, *He has a nice voice . . . talks like anybody else . . .*

"I'm Harley Juster."

. . . good-looking, all that dark hair. . . . It looks normal. . . .

Harley Juster's eyebrows went up. "And your name is — ?"

How embarrassing. He was reminding me of my manners. "Ami. Ami Pelter."

He put out his hand. It was a perfect little man's hand. Short fingers, pink nails, dark hairs growing along the knuckles. We shook hands. My big hand swallowed up his little hand.

"Why're you going to New Castle, Ami?"

"To visit my mother." I hoped he wouldn't ask why my mother lived one place and I lived someplace else.

"So what do you do, Ami?"

"I go to school."

He nodded and smiled. He looked like he was

waiting for me to say something else. Suddenly I got it. "What do you do, Mr. Juster?"

"Call me Harley. I work in radio, Ami. Do you ever listen to WYME?"

"Yes."

"I'm surprised you don't recognize my voice." He thrust his neck around inside his collar and said, "Boys and girls! It's hit time with — "

"Oh!" All of a sudden I knew who he was. "You're — "

" — haaard-hitting Haaarley!"

"You're famous!"

"Well. . . ." He smiled.

We talked all the way to New Castle. He told me how he got into his radio career. He said he'd been working in radio for almost twenty years. "You don't just get your own show because you want it. You have to pay your dues. I've done all the little jobs, I've done everything, and never made much money, either. It's the glory you're there for, in radio, not the money. I persisted because it was my dream to have my own show, and finally I got it five years ago."

"That's wonderful, Mr. Juster." Now that I knew he was famous, I felt sort of shy, but at the same time he was so nice it was really easy to talk to him. Just before we got to New Castle, he asked me if I'd like to make any special request for his show on Monday. At first I thought about Mia and me and Robert. Then I had a better idea. I asked him to play "I Still Love

You," by The Secrets and say it was for Fred and Jan.

"Special friends?"

"My brother and his girlfriend."

"Very good, and you want the usual? Dedicated to Fred and Jan from Ami?"

"Could you say, from a secret friend?"

Harley smiled. "Sure."

"New Castle next," the bus driver called. "New Castle coming up fast, folks."

I started getting my things together. Then I thought of something else. "Would you mind giving me your autograph?" I found a piece of paper and he wrote, "To Ami, a new friend. With all best wishes from Harley Juster." I thanked him and we shook hands.

I stood up as the bus pulled into the station. I saw Mom through the window. Tallest woman in the crowd. I get my size from her. She's taller than my father, just like Jan is taller than Fred. Come to think of it, Ms. Linsley is taller than Dad.

When Mom was living home, I never thought about what she looked like. She was there, she was my mom. Now, whenever I see her, it's just like looking at a picture of someone I recognize, someone I know that I know, but who I don't remember all the little details about, and yet I *do* remember. I know that sounds strange. But that's the best way I can explain it.

Also, Mom does look a little different now

because one, she cut her hair, and two, she lost some weight and changed the way she dresses. She used to just wear jeans and T-shirts or old shirts of my father's around the house. "I'm comfortable," she used to say. But I guess she can't dress that way now that she's got a job. Or maybe she doesn't like to, anymore. Today she was wearing wide, green corduroy slacks and a light purple blouse, one of those Indian-looking blouses, with embroidery around the neck, and long silver earrings. She looked beautiful! She was standing with her hands in her pockets, watching the people come out of the bus.

She saw me right away. "Ami!" She came forward, a big stride, a big smile, her arms out. "Ami!"

"Hi, Mom." We hugged; it was sort of awkward, arms and elbows. My throat was tight and my smile felt tight, too. We both started talking at once. "I had such a great trip, I met this neat man — "

"Are you hungry?"

" — works in radio — "

"We could go out. Pizza or — "

" — and he's so small, really teeny, but after you talk to him for a few minutes — "

" — or go to my place, whichever you — "

Then we both stopped at the same moment. Mom leaned over me and sniffed. "You've been biting your hair." She hugged me again, harder, and then she stood back and looked at me. "Oh, it's so good to see you, honey. I've missed you a lot."

All of a sudden, tears came up into my eyes. We walked to Mom's car, holding hands.

Chapter 10

"He fell down the stairs?" Mom said. Her cheeseburger stopped halfway to her mouth. "Martin? *Martin* fell down the stairs? Was he drinking? Martin doesn't drink!"

I looked around the restaurant. Mom's voice carries. "Mom, Dad doesn't drink."

"That's what I just said."

"And he didn't fall down a *whole* flight of stairs. Just two or three."

"But I always thought he was really well co-ordinated. He skis in winter and — how did it happen? How did he do that?"

I was sorry I'd said anything. "Well, uh . . . he was running after me."

"Running after you?" She leaned across the little red table. "Honey, he's not getting abusive, is he? Ami — " She grabbed my hand in both of hers. "Ami, you'd tell me, wouldn't you?"

"Mom! I can't believe you'd say a thing like that about Dad."

Now she looked embarrassed. "Well, he was awfully angry at me, and a lot of times people take their anger out on the wrong person. I see it all the time in my work."

"Dad hardly ever gets mad."

"That's just the way it looks to you. Look, I want to say something. I left your father because, well — I had to. I mean, for my own sanity. Maybe that's hard for you to understand, but your father and I — we tried to keep things smooth. Smooth on the surface. Your father's idea, if you want to know the truth. He can't stand a little controversy, just keep everything nice and quiet, that's his idea. Raise your voice a single decibel and he thinks it's a declaration of war."

I fiddled with the straps of my knapsack. I wished she wouldn't start on this.

"And you know why I didn't take you with me. God knows, I would have loved to! But your father put his foot down. I could leave, but without you kids. He wasn't letting go of you."

I looked up. "What?"

Mom nodded. "But the more important thing is, I couldn't take you because I don't have two cents to rub together. This job really pays peanuts. Anyway, I think Martin was right about

71

it being better for you to stay in your own home — "

"Okay, I know."

" — where you've lived practically all your life. The stability thing. It wouldn't have been the greatest idea to yank you away from all your friends and — "

"I know all that, Mom, it's *okay*." I don't think she was listening to me.

"But here's what I want to say: If, *ever*, anything happens that makes it bad for you, you come to me, Ami. Sweetie. You know you can do that, don't you? You would, wouldn't you?"

I nodded.

"You're not trapped. Never feel that way. You can always come live with me."

"You haven't got room for me to live with you."

She sighed. "I know. That little closet where I live. It's not bad, really, kind of cozy. That's what I tell myself, since it's all I can afford. Listen — " She suddenly smiled. Mom's like that, she goes from dead serious to smiles in one second.

"I'm going out on a limb to make a prediction. Are you ready? Your mother's going to be a great, big, fat success in her work. I'm going to get promoted and all that good stuff, and make some decent money. Then I'll get a real place, an apartment with a room for you and a room for me — "

She took my hand. "Ami? Are you happy? Are you okay? I want so much for you to be happy, honey. I don't know . . . maybe that's foolish. Everybody can't be happy all the time. I should know. And I should know I can't live your life for you. Nobody can live your life for you, except you." Then she said, very emphatically, "You can't depend on other people for your happiness," and she stared at me seriously. "Will you remember that?"

I nodded and we both went back to eating our cheeseburgers. Suddenly, I said, "Mom? Remember Unccy Bernard?"

"My brother?"

"No. Unccy Bernard."

"Your uncle Bernard? He's my brother, Ami."

"Mom. *Unccy Bernard*. My yellow bear that *Uncle* Bernard sent me when — "

"Oh!" She clapped herself on the forehead. "What's the matter with me? Unccy Bernard! Of course. How could I forget Unccy Bernard? He didn't fall down the stairs, did he?"

"Mom!"

She laughed and rubbed my head. "But, listen, you still didn't tell me what happened to Martin. Why was he chasing you? Where did this happen? At home?"

"No. We were visiting someone and — " I stirred the straw around in my shake. It was too complicated to explain. "You see, we were eating supper there and Dad was laughing a lot, and

Forrest's obnoxious nephew was there, so I was sort of feeling not so great, and then when she brought out the strawberry shortcake — " I stopped. I wasn't doing this very well!

If Unccy Bernard were here, he would say it for me. *You see, my good friend, Ami's a sensitive girl, even though her family doesn't appreciate that. But there was her daddy, forgetting he was married; there was Ms. Linsley in her ballet slippers, and there was the Biggest Flirt, Jones. . . . It was just too much for Ami. Now do you understand?*

"I'm a little confused," Mom said. "You were visiting someone with a nephew named Forrest?"

"No, Mom, the nephew was Jones. Forrest is Ms. Linsley, our science teacher."

"Linsley? Linsley? I don't remember her."

"She just started teaching last year, right when you moved away."

"Oh, so I don't know her. I thought I knew all your teachers. Okay, so she's a friend of your father's?"

I reached under the table and pulled up my socks. "She says she's my friend, too. Last year — "

"What? I can't hear you when you're under the table like that."

I sat up straight. "My friend, too." I said loudly. "Last year, she and I talked a lot. When you moved out."

"You did? The two of you talked a lot?" Mom's

74

eyes got red around the rims. "What did you talk about?"

"You know. Just — things."

"Oh." Mom sat there for a moment, then she started pulling the cover off a creamer the wrong way. Cream squirted out onto her hands. "I always do that," she said. "What did you two talk about? Me? Did you talk about me?"

"No, Mom." I opened two creamers and poured them into her coffee.

"You're so good at that." She gave me a sweet look, as if I'd done something special for her. She wiped her eyes. "Oh, I'm getting teary! Don't mind me, sweetie. I miss you, and — no, no, no, no, Pat, you are not going to get started on that." She wiped her eyes again and smiled. "Anyway. So you were visiting this teacher — okay, then what?"

"Well, we were eating supper and, and, I wanted some fresh air. So I went outside and took a walk, and then I found a phone booth and called Mia."

"And your father ran after you and that's when he fell down the stairs? Why'd he run after you? I don't get it."

"I guess Dad got sort of upset. You know, because I left like that, in the middle of the dessert. And — "

Mom gave a little snort of laughter. "Maybe he thought it was instant replay. First, his wife walks out on him, then his daughter."

"The steps are old and crummy. It wasn't his fault. He's using a cane now. Someone said it makes him look like a war hero."

Mom's eyebrows went up. "Really! Was that someone Ms. Linsley? By the way, is that what Martin calls her? Ms. Linsley?"

"Mom! I told you they're friends."

"Sorry, Ami. I'm being juvenile."

"Her name is Forrest Lake Linsley."

"Pretty name." She pushed crumbs around on the table.

Was Mom jealous? Could you not want to live with someone and still be jealous?

"Well, I guess we should leave," Mom said, in her more normal voice. "You need anything, Ami? A new bra?" She laughed. "Ami, remember this? 'My voice has matured, but my chest hasn't.'"

Mom and I made up that joke last year, when I was going crazy, because everybody had more on their chests than I did. Now, it's sort of the opposite.

Mom took my hand and gave me another sweet look. "You know what, Ami? It's not true, though, about your voice. You had that wonderful deep voice even when you were a little kid. It was the cutest thing! This little toddler with the big voice. People used to stop me and say, 'That little girl is adorable. What a voice.'"

I wished she'd go on talking about when I was a baby. I really liked hearing it. "What else?"

Mom linked fingers with me. "Should I tell you all the cute things you did when you were a toddler? I have millions of stories!"

"Okay."

"Okay! Okay, she says. Miss Cool! Doesn't care if I tell her or not." She looked at me. "How do you do that, Ami?"

"Do *what*?"

"Come across so self-contained. I know this isn't true honey, but sometimes it seems like things don't touch you."

I didn't know what to say. Did she think I didn't care about things, didn't get hurt inside? *That* hurt me, but for some reason I just smiled. "You going to tell me stories about when I was a little kid?"

"I could."

"I really want to hear them, Mom."

"Good. I like people who really *want*. Who really care."

Chapter 11

New Castle, where Mom lives, is a really small town. It's surrounded on all sides by fields and farms. Everywhere you go in town, you can smell the farms, sort of a hay-ey, barny smell. Mom rents an apartment in a big old house with a huge front porch. A lot of people used to live in that house, a family with seven kids, but now there's just one old lady, Mrs. Hagadorn, and her cat.

Mrs. Hagadorn's son made Mom's apartment out of a couple of rooms on one side of the house, so Mrs. Hagadorn could have some extra income and not have to leave her home. That seems sensible, but what I wonder is why he didn't make the apartment any bigger. It's incredibly small. Mom's main room is the living room. There's a closet (her only one), some shelves for books and things, a pull-out couch which is also her bed, a couple of lamps, and a portable TV. She doesn't have a table; she eats with a tray on her lap or sitting on the couch.

Her kitchen is more like a little hall with a tiny fridge and a little stove and a few cupboards. It's true she has everything she needs in there, but the two of us can't go in together without bumping into each other.

And the bathroom — I couldn't believe it the first time I walked in. You open the door, take two steps, and that's it. No sink, no tub, no linen closet. A showerhead comes out of the wall over the toilet. If you want to shower, you just pull the curtain, which is bunched against the wall. The water runs out through a drain in the middle of the floor. The only things to get wet are the toilet, which doesn't matter, and the toilet paper, which is in a metal container. "Cute, isn't it?" Mom said, the first time I visited her. "They thought of everything."

"This entire place could fit into my closet," I said now. She had stuff stacked everywhere and books and plants crowded on the windowsills. I went around looking at the pictures on the walls. Lots of pictures of me and Fred, and some stuff cut out of newspapers and magazines. There were a few I hadn't seen before. One was of a flock of birds flying up out of a field. "Why'd you put this up?" I said.

Mom was on her hands and knees, rummaging through a cardboard box. "The birds? No special reason, it just appealed to me."

Another newspaper picture she'd put up showed a long line of farmers on tractors. Underneath it said, "Farmers from all over the country came together in the capital Tuesday to protest indifference to their plight." When I think of farmers I automatically think of men, but there were plenty of women. The farmer on the head tractor was a woman wearing jeans, a frilly blouse, and earrings.

Mom sat back on her heels, waving two cloth napkins. "Found them! You see, we go in style around here. Bring in the tray, Ami."

We'd been out shopping all afternoon. On the way home, we picked up some Chinese takeout. I put the tray with the food on one of the cardboard boxes. Mom put down the folded cloth napkins and silverware. We sat on the floor on either side of the box. "There we are," Mom said. "Elegance at home."

"Do you mind being poor?"

She broke open an egg roll. "I don't love it, but I guess, for me, it's a trade-off I'm willing to make. I'm independent now, practically for the first time in my life, and I love that, Ami. And I'm doing work I really, really like." She passed me one of the little boxes. "Take some more rice, Ami."

"Thanks, it tastes great. . . . Do you read all those books?"

"Ohhh." Mom sighed, as if she were really exhausted. "I'm still trying to catch up with all the literature in the field. I didn't work for so many years I got left behind in a lot of — "

The phone rang. I started to get up to answer it, but Mom made a little motion with her hand and went into the kitchen. "Hello?" she said. "Oh, hi!"

I didn't eavesdrop on purpose, but I couldn't help hearing everything. "Sure, that sounds good. . . . Uh-huh. . . . When? Wednesday?" She laughed. "Oh, for you, Danny, yes!"

Danny? Who was he? Was that why she didn't want me to answer the phone? On a TV show I'd seen the week before, a woman fell in love with a guy in college. All her kids were grown up, so she must have been at least forty-five. The guy wasn't that much older than Fred. Then I thought how, without Fred and me around, Mom could do anything she wanted. Without us, she didn't have to be a mother.

She came back, sat down, and started eating again. "I luuuv Chinese food," she said, scraping out one of the little boxes. She seemed to be in a really good mood, not tired anymore. She didn't say anything about the phone call.

Suddenly I said, "I don't know how you stand it here, Mom. I mean, this little rinky-dink town. The whole place smells like cow flops."

"You smell manure because there are a lot of farms around here," Mom said. Her voice got a frosty edge. I hate it when her voice gets like

81

that. "A lot of hard-working farmers, hard-working men and women. Good people. And they're having big problems these days. You see that picture on the wall? I put it up for a reason. Just so I wouldn't get smug or forgetful. The farmers are over their heads in debt; some of them are losing farms that have been in their families for a hundred years. Do you know what that means? Do you know what this country would be like without the men and women who run the little farms?"

She went on like that. I was embarrassed and really mad. Maybe it was a stupid thing to say, but she didn't have to get up on a soapbox. "May I turn on the TV?" I said, when she finally wound down.

"Certainly."

We watched TV and ate apples for dessert. Mom kept burping. It was pretty disgusting. "I guess that food was too oily for me," she said. I didn't say anything. I was still pretty mad about the big lecture she gave me. When the news came on, I went into the bathroom and took a long shower.

The couch was open when I came out. "Clean sheets in your honor." Mom sat on the edge of the bed in her pajamas, brushing her hair. "I'm bushed." She shut off the light and got in beside me. "Ami. . . ." She sort of murmured it. "Sweetie . . . glad you're here." In about two seconds she was asleep.

I didn't fall asleep right away. Being in bed next to Mom reminded me of when I was little. If I had a bad dream, I would run down the hall from my bedroom and get in bed with her and Dad, but always on her side. I wanted to be next to Mommy. Sometimes, she would let me sleep the whole night right there. I hadn't done that in years.

I listened to her breathe. I used to do that, too, when I was little, lie there and listen to her breathe, my hand on her shoulder or her arm.

I touched her. I put my hand on her shoulder. Her skin was warm. I snuggled up next to her. She still smelled like tangerines. I was almost asleep when I thought, If Mom was still home, still living with Dad, I would never have had this chance to sleep in the same bed with her again.

Chapter 12

The day after I got back from visiting Mom, I was going to go home with Mia after school, but her mother was waiting outside in the car. "Mia!" She stuck her hand out the window. "Over here."

The baby was strapped in the car seat in back, sucking on a bottle of juice. Mrs. Jenson was wearing blue running pants and a gray sweat-shirt with a hood. "Hi, Mrs. Jenson," I said, "have you been running?"

She laughed. "This is my disguise, Ami, so I look athletic. Raking leaves, actually." Then she looked at Mia and frowned. "You have a dentist appointment. You were supposed to get excused fifteen minutes early."

Mia groaned and grabbed my hand. We both go to the same dentist, Morton Gage. Mia really hates dentists. She says the sound of the drill in her mouth, even when she's full of novocaine, makes her so nervous she wants to scream.

"Plus," she says, "his jokes. Why did the Little Moron jump off the Empire State Building, Mia? I don't know, Doctor Gage, why? To see if he had guts, Mia, ha ha ha!"

"Get in the car," her mother said, "and don't be so dramatic."

Mia slammed the door. "See you tomorrow, Ami, if I'm not dead."

I was almost home, taking my time, before I remembered that Harley Juster was going to dedicate a song to Fred and Jan on his radio program today. I ran the rest of the way. I only hoped Fred came home early, so I could see his face when Harley Juster said, "This is 'I Still Love You' for Fred and Jan."

The back door was unlocked. Good, I thought, Fred's home. "Fred?" I kicked off my sneakers and stopped dead. There was a stranger, a man, sitting in our kitchen. He had long hair and a guitar slung around his neck. He acted like he belonged here. "Rooootie tootie . . . ," he sang, "roootie tootie, who's this cutie?"

Maybe he was in the wrong house. A lot of the houses on our street resemble each other. Once, when Fred was a little boy, he went into another white house with black shutters, sat down in the living room, and watched an entire show before anyone noticed him.

Maybe I was in the wrong house. No, I

couldn't be. Alcott was curled up on the stranger's lap.

"Hi," he said. "Greetings. Shalom." He had a curved silver earring like the letter C in one ear.

I stood by the door. "Who are you?"

"Who am I?" He sang, "Hi, I'm Bill, if you will . . . rootie tootie. . . . And who are you . . . big tall cutie?" The earring flashed.

"How'd you get in here?"

"Same way you did." He leaned back on two legs of the chair.

"Stop that! You'll break the chair." Why did I say that? He could be a murderer, escaped convict, a thief. Anything!

He let the chair down, and Alcott jumped off his lap. "Roootie toootie . . . chair legs on the floor . . . ask me something more. . . ."

Even if he wasn't a criminal, he was crazy. I looked over at the cupboard. The knife Dad had used this morning to cut bread was still on the cutting board. "You better get out of here."

"Why?" he said.

I took a step toward the cupboard. "You don't belong here." I grabbed the knife.

He looked at the knife, open-mouthed. "Do we have a little communication problem here? I'm Bill Shank. Friend of Fred. Are you his sister?"

"How do I know you're Fred's friend?"

He didn't take his eyes off the knife. "Don't get excited. I came home with Fred and Jan."

86

"Where are they?"

"They went out to get some pizza."

That was the first thing that made sense to me. "What'd you say your name was?"

"Bill Shank. And you're — "

"Ami," I said.

"Right. I've heard Fred talk about you. Listen, Ami, how would you like to put that knife back where it belongs? It's making me sort of nervous." He leaned back on the chair legs again, then straightened up. "Oh, sorry about that. Bad habit."

I put the knife down. Now I was sort of embarrassed. "I thought — "

" — that I was some space cadet who battered down the kitchen door? Ami! Couldn't you tell by looking at me what a harmless guy I am? I don't even kill flies. I'm not kidding, I capture them and set them free outdoors."

I sat down at the other end of the table, still being cautious. "You do?"

"I figure that fly is here for some reason."

"Flies carry diseases."

"Well, that's true. But, still, there's got to be a reason why they exist. Right? It makes for an interesting ethical question, Ami."

We started talking about when, if ever, it's okay to take life. It's really horrible to think about how many creatures we kill for food, to begin with, and then for sport and for things like fur coats and shoes and wallets.

"Not to mention the animals we just run down

with our cars," Bill said. "You ever go on a trip and notice them, Ami? Sometimes I think, what if all those dead animals by the side of the road were human beings. Wow! Everyone would be going crazy, screaming and yelling. But the way we figure now, oh, it's just another animal. Like that animal's life doesn't mean a thing." He said he became a vegetarian when he started thinking about things like that. "Ami, you got me started on my second favorite subject. Don't let me stop you from whatever you have to do."

"Only homework. What's your first favorite subject?"

He held up his guitar. "One guess." He went into the living room to wait for Fred.

I opened my math book, then I just sat there listening to Bill playing the guitar. I finally did the first set of problems. I had Robert's name written all over the inside cover of my notebook. Robert Volz. Ten letters. Bill's name was nine letters. Three, three times. Maybe I'd call Mia, later. Maybe I'd tell her about Bill. *Mia*, I'd say, *this really interesting person —*

A silver earring, Ami? Gimme a break!

Mia, it's narrow-minded to judge a person by the things he wears. And by the way, did you ever think about how many animals human beings kill?

I was figuring out what Mia would say, when Fred and Jan came in, each of them carrying a big white pizza box. That reminded me of Harley Juster's program. I hoped I hadn't missed it. I jumped up and turned on the radio.

Jan put her pizza down on the cupboard. "Hi, Ami."

"Hi, Jan." I turned up the sound on the radio.

"I'm making supper, Ami, so you do the salad," Fred said. He lit the oven and put the pizzas in.

"Why can't you make the salad?" When it's his turn to do supper, he always finds something for me to do.

"You know you make better salads than I do, Ami." He pronounced it in the French way, Ahmee, so that it meant love, or something like that. And he gave me one of his special, great smiles.

"Don't let this guy con you, Ami," Jan said. "Make him do the work himself."

"Whose side are you on?" Fred bumped into Jan.

"In this case, your sister's." She bumped him back.

And just then, Harley Juster said in his excited radio voice, "And *now* I have a special request for — FRED AND JAN! Fred and Jan, are you out there listening, you two lovebirds?"

Fred and Jan looked at each other. "Us?" Jan said. "Did you call in, Fred?"

"No. Did you?"

I thought they would guess. I thought they would both turn to me and say, "Ami must have done it!"

" 'I Still Love You,' for Jan and Fred, FROM A SECRET, SPECIAL FRIEND! And, naturally, the tune is by . . . THE SECRETS!"

The song began. I was sure my face would give me away, but Jan and Fred never guessed. They kept looking at each other all through the song. Jan pointed at Fred. "You devil!" He shook his head and grinned and pointed back at her. "Not me," she said. "I didn't do it." When the song came to an end, they kissed. It was perfect!

A few minutes later, Bill came in. Fred asked him if he wanted to stay to supper. "I never turn down food," Bill said. "How you doing, Ami?"

"Oh, you and Ami met?" Fred said.

Bill winked and looked over at the cupboard where I'd left the knife. "We sure did. Some interesting meeting!"

Was he going to tell about the knife? I grabbed my books and ran up the stairs. Behind me, I could hear the three of them talking, Bill's voice, then Fred and Jan laughing. I ran down the hall to my room and threw myself down on my bed with Unccy Bernard. I knew Bill was telling Fred and Jan what a fool I'd been.

Unccy patted my face. "Ami, sweetheart." Then he patted his own face. "Unccy, sweetheart." He flopped his head against me. "Ha ha ha, Ami? Unccy Bernard made a funny."

"I don't feel like laughing right now, Unccy."

He put his paw to his forehead. "Thinking, you know. Have to make Ami laugh. Have to say something funny. Are you ready? What kind of dog doesn't have a tail?" Unccy patted my arm. "Tough one. Take your time. What kind of dog doesn't have a tail? Give up? Hot dog!"

"Oh, Unccy."

"Tee hee hee," he coaxed.

"Tee hee hee."

"Thank you, my little sweetheart." He flopped his head against my chest, and we lay down together.

A few moments later, there was a tap at the door and Jan looked in. I pushed Unccy under the covers. "Fred wants to know if you're going to make that salad, Ami." She came in and sat down on the bed. "How was your visit with your mom?"

"It was good."

"Maybe I'll go with Fred when he visits her next week. Do you think she'd mind?"

"No." I sat up. Jan was looking really happy. Because of the song? If I hadn't felt so miserable about Bill telling on me, I would have felt like Cinderella's fairy godmother. Could you really make people happy that easily?

"The only thing is, Mom doesn't have room for anybody. Fred just sleeps in a sleeping bag on the floor when he goes."

"Well, I could do that, too. I'll take my sleeping bag. It would be neat to see your mom again."

I got up and started brushing my hair. "Jan?

Did Bill, um, say anything about a knife?"

Jan piled her hair on top of her head and looked at herself in the mirror. "Not that I remember."

I put my brush down. "He didn't?"

"A knife? What about it?"

"Oh . . . nothing, really. Tell Fred I'll be right down. I have to make a phone call."

I went across the hall to my parents' room and sat down on Mom's side of the bed. I called Mia. "Hi!"

"Hi. Why'd you call?" She sounded really grumpy.

"To see if you survived Doctor Gage."

"No, I didn't. Anything else you want to know?"

"Did you get a shot?"

"I don't want to talk about it!"

It didn't seem like this conversation was going to go anywhere, so I told her about Harley Juster and the song and said I'd see her tomorrow.

Downstairs, Fred was making one of his special desserts, dumping yogurt, bananas, raisins, and apples into the blender.

Jan was setting the table. I tore apart a head of lettuce. Bill scraped a carrot. "Roootie toootie," he hummed. He looked at me and winked.

Chapter 13

That week Robert was absent three days from school. "I wonder what's wrong with him?" Mia said.

"He probably has a cold. Everybody has a cold." I blew my nose.

"Maybe we should do something. Call him up. Maybe he's depressed because he's sick. He might really need cheering up."

"Right, Mia. We'll get on the phone and say, 'Hello, Robert, this is the well-known, famous Society for Cheering Sick People.' Then we'll tell him one of Doctor Gage's Little Moron jokes. 'Robert, why did the Little Moron take straw to bed with him?' 'I don't know, Mia, why?' 'To feed his nightmare, ha ha ha.' "

"We could just say, 'This is Ami and Mia.' "

"Good idea, Mia, if you don't have a heart attack first."

On Friday, Robert was back in school. I heard him telling Miles that he'd had a sore throat. Which I told Mia. "Oh, thank goodness," she said. "I was so worried about him!" I thought it was just Mia being Mia, which means Mia being excessive.

Saturday, Fred left early in the morning with Jan to go see Mom. Later, Ms. Linsley came by for Dad in her red VW and, even though it was raining, they went to a football game. I called Mia, but she couldn't come over. "My mother's forcing me to do housework today. She says I better learn sometime."

I thought vaguely about cleaning up our house. It was pretty messy. Dad has us vacuum and wipe things up every couple of weeks, but he isn't a bear on housework. But what if Mom came home right now? She'd say, "Look at this place! Hasn't anybody done anything since I left?"

I dragged out the vacuum cleaner, but then I didn't even plug it in. Mom wasn't coming home, at least not this weekend. Right now, in fact, she was probably showing Jan around her place, showing her the shower, and how if two people went into the kitchen at the same time, they tripped over each other. And she would be laughing and rubbing Fred's head and saying how much she missed him and how glad she was he'd come down to visit her.

The house was quiet with just me and Alcott in it. I tried not to, but I kept thinking about next spring when Fred would be in France and it would be just Dad and me. I'd probably be home alone a lot. I started to really depress myself. "Boo hoo, Ami!" I said in a loud voice.

I went upstairs to my room and danced around for a while with Unccy Bernard, then we sang some old Brownie camp songs. "Kookaburra sits in the old gum tree-eee, merry merry king of the bushes, he-eee." After that, I turned on the TV in the living room and the radio in the kitchen and baked a batch of butterscotch chip cookies. They came out really good and I ate most of them myself. Then I sewed a button on one of my blouses and washed my hair. It was raining hard outside. I put on all the lights and it was cozy in the house.

Around four o'clock Mia called. "Did you see what it's doing out there? It's pouring buckets! Cats and dogs! Worms and fishes! Did you do anything fun today?"

"I baked butterscotch cookies. How about you? Can you come over now?"

"No, we're going out for pizza at that new pizza place on Burleigh Road. My dad did the electrical wiring and when they paid him, they gave him coupons for about twelve free pizza dinners, too! He says let's take advantage before they go out of business."

"Why are they going out of business?"

"They aren't. That's just my father's idea of a

hilarious joke. He and Doctor Gage should get together. Have you been alone all day?"

"Yes."

"Poor Ami!"

"It's okay."

"No, it isn't. I think it's terrible that your father didn't take you with him."

"No, thanks, Mia! I don't want to spend the day with him and Ms. Linsley."

"Well, I hope he has a big fat guilty conscience. I bet he does! Call me tomorrow, okay?"

After I hung up, I watched TV and ate the rest of the butterscotch cookies with ice cream and chocolate sauce. There was a rerun of M*A*S*H on. I love Alan Alda; I think he's incredibly sexy, even if he is pretty old.

I was still watching TV when Dad came home. He limped to the couch and bent over to kiss me. He smelled like cold air and hot dogs. "Hi, honey, how're things? Everything okay?"

"Sure," I said, "fine," but the moment I said it, I felt like crying. It was awful. I'd been perfectly all right until Dad walked in.

"Well! What a football game," he said.

"I don't want to hear about it." My voice was choked. I ran up to my room and stayed in there the rest of the evening. Dad tried to talk to me, but I said I was just tired and I didn't want to talk.

Sunday morning, he knocked on my door.

"Are you up, Ami? How about breakfast at the Bagel Tree? You, me, and Mia."

I couldn't believe it. I love going there, but Dad is usually too cheap to eat out, even for Sunday breakfast. He always says the same thing — what you spend on one meal in a restaurant would feed our family for a week.

Mia's father answered the phone when I called. Mr. Jenson is a really big, really quiet man. Sometimes you can be in Mia's house and not even know Mr. Jenson is there, because he's just quietly reading or thinking. "I'm sure it's okay, Ami," he said, in his quiet voice.

Then Mia got on the phone. "The Bagel Tree? Me, too? I told you your father would have a guilty conscience, Ami."

When we walked into the Bagel Tree and smelled fresh bagels, we just inhaled. "Fabulous," Mia breathed. We got in line. There's always a huge crowd on Sunday mornings. Sometimes you have to wait half an hour for a table, but Mia and I don't mind. We like to read the bulletin board, especially the personal ads. We have this sort of game we play, where we each take an ad, read it out loud, and try to say something witty about it. Mia is generally better at it than I am.

"TWO CAREER WOMEN WITH CONSIDERATE, WARM, PERKY PERSONALITIES LOOKING FOR SIMILAR ROOMMATE TO SHARE TOWNHOUSE," I read.

97

"Not a chance, Ami," Mia said, sadly. "Not unless we clone ourselves."

It was her turn. "WANTED, HOUSEBROKEN DOG, NO MONEY, BUT HEART FULL OF LOVE FOR RIGHT POOCH."

"Remember, he has to get along with Alcott," I said.

"You mean — !" Mia looked alarmed. "He has to like chipmunk steak?"

My father turned to look at us. "Do you two gigglers know what you're going to order?"

There were at least six people working behind the counter. A fat black girl in a pink apron waited on us. Her skin was beautiful, the color of creamy chocolate. She wore a pink cap that said LET THEM EAT BAGELS. "Next! What'll it be, girls?"

Mia and I both ordered a large orange juice, hot chocolate, and four bagels to share — rye, sesame, whole wheat, and chocolate.

"You guys are hungry this morning," the girl behind the counter said.

"Chocolate bagels?" my father said. "I can't believe anybody in her right mind would eat a chocolate bagel."

"Dad, it's an experience. Like cohoe salmon."

There was no place for us all to sit down together. Mia and I found a window table and my father found a single in back, across from a boy with a guitar. For a minute I thought it was Bill and I had this really odd, quivery sensation in the back of my neck.

"Sssst! Ami!" Mia nodded at a man at the counter. His back was straight as a flagpole. He was wearing a white jacket with gold buttons and a white cap with gold braid. "Commodore Whitesides," Mia said. "He parked his boat down the street."

Next, we watched a boy and girl outside on the sidewalk. They were saying good-bye, touching hands, walking away, and then coming back and touching hands again. They were both wearing white jeans and corduroy jackets, but her jacket was huge, the sleeves went way down over her hands, and his was so small his wrists stuck out. "I bet they're wearing each other's jackets," Mia said. "That's so romantic!"

And just then, Robert walked in with a girl. "Who is she? She's so cute," Mia whimpered.

The girl was short, redheaded like Robert, with freckles. She was wearing a blue vest.

I leaned across the table. "Mia, it must be his sister. They have the same exact hair. His sister, or maybe a cousin."

At the back of the room, my father half stood up and looked over at us to see if we were ready to go. I held up my cocoa cup to show him I was still drinking.

Robert and the girl were talking, but they kept looking back at the door, as if they were waiting for someone. I thought maybe he saw us. He took off his glasses and hooked them over the collar of his rugby shirt.

"Don't you love that shirt?" Mia said. "He

looks so cute without his glasses, he ought to get contacts."

"I like him better with the glasses."

"I like him anyway!"

A tall man came in and went over to stand with Robert and the girl. The girl took something out of her pocket and gave it to the man.

"His father," Mia guessed. "You must be right, Ami, that's his sister." She looked really relieved.

"Want some more cocoa?" I asked Mia.

"If we go up to the counter, he'll see us!"

"I think he did, already."

"Ami!" Mia flung her head down on her arms.

"He's looking this way."

She sat right up and we both looked out the window, pretending to be watching something really interesting outside.

Then my father was standing there. "Okay, girls, ready?"

Mia and I got up. Neither one of us even dared look over at Robert.

Chapter 14

That week, somehow or other, Mia and I decided we should write Robert a letter. We went to her house after school. Her mother was just leaving with Sara for a doctor's appointment.

"Is Sara sick, Mrs. Jenson?" She didn't look sick. She was bouncing up and down in Mrs. Jenson's arm and drooling all over herself and Mrs. Jenson.

"Just a check up, Ami. You know, the usual — "

"Little Sara!" Mia tugged at her sister's foot. "Give your Mia a biig smile!" Sara got this goofy smile on her face.

"Mia," her mother said, "you're going to de-foot Sara in a moment." She put the baby in the car seat. "Tell your sister I said to clean up her room before I get home."

"She won't listen to me."

"Well, tell her, anyway. And you do your room, too, it's getting to look like the town dump again."

"I don't have the time. Ami and I have something to do."

"If it's homework, okay. But if it's going goo goo over some boy in school, forget it." Mrs. Jenson backed out of the driveway.

"Come on, Ami!" Mia slammed the front door behind us. "Do you believe my mother? *Goo goo? Defoot* Sara? She is bizarre."

We made ice cream sodas and took them upstairs to Mia's room. "What's wrong with this room?" Mia said. She picked up a pile of clothes from the floor and threw them into the closet. "Do you think this room needs cleaning, Ami? Give me your honest opinion."

I sat down in the rocking chair. "I like your room."

Mia shoved a pile of magazines off the bed. "Thank you. I do, too. My mother is a fanatic about cleaning! Does your mother make you crazy over cleaning up stuff — " She stopped. "I am a dope!" She leaned over me, her hands on the arms of the rocker and rocked me back and forth. "Did I make you feel bad saying that?"

"It's okay, you don't have to be so sensitive about me."

102

"Yes, I do. You're my best friend, I don't want to hurt your feelings."

"Mia, it's okay to talk about my mother. She's not dead or anything. She just moved to another town."

Mia rocked me harder. "Are you absolutely sure?" She rocked me so hard I almost went over backwards. Then she lost her balance and fell on top of me. We started laughing. Mia was going, "Hee hee hee." And I was going, "Whoops! Whoops! Whoops!"

"Isn't that adorable." Stacey was standing in the doorway, peering in with her long nose. "The two little witches are at it again." She came in and sat down on the bed. "What did you guys have in these glasses?"

"Poison brew," Mia said.

"Smells good. Any left over?"

"You want some of our poison, Stacey, darling? You're not afraid of witches' brew?"

Stacey smiled. She looked pretty when she smiled. "Can I borrow your green jumper for tomorrow?" she asked Mia.

"I told you, you can borrow anything you want."

"That's because almost nothing of yours fits me."

"Thanks for the thanks," Mia said, throwing the green jumper at her sister. "Now, will you kindly leave, so Ami and I can do our homework?"

Stacey strolled out, taking her time. As soon as she left, Mia and I began our letter to Robert. "Keep it simple," Mia said.

I wrote, *Dear Robert, We are your secret admirers. We think you're very handsome and, in fact, we love you. Love, the Secret Two Society.*

Mia looked over my shoulder. "It's basically good," she said in a kind way.

"Which means, you think it's terrible."

"N-n-n-no! Just, we should make it more emotional. Let me add some stuff."

She took the notebook and wrote, *Dear, Darling, Beloved Robert, We are your secret admirers. We think you're very handsome and, in fact, we adore you. We love your red hair. We love everything about you, even your gray and white rugby shirt! Double Love from your devoted admirers, The STS (Secret Two Society), aka the IRVFS (International Robert Volz Fan Society).*

"It's great, Mia."

"You don't think it's overdone?"

I waved my hand in the air. "Maybe a touch. But then, again, maybe it's absolutely perfect. Anyway, since we're not going to mail it — "

"Who says?"

"What do you mean, who says? We can't mail *that*. To his *house*? That's crazy. His mother might open it, or his sister, or — "

"If we're not sending it, why'd we write it, Ami?"

"Because."

"Because what?"

"Because we wanted to."

"Good reason," Mia said.

"Right."

"Suppose we put it in his desk at school? Print PRIVATE on the envelope and — "

"Mia. What if Miles sees it? Or Alex? Or a teacher?"

"What's a teacher doing snooping in Robert's desk?"

"The point is, we're not going to get away with it, Mia. There're just too many people around. Somebody'll see us, for sure."

Mia put some music on her tape deck so she could think better. "I know. We hire somebody to deliver it to him. Personal messenger service."

I thought about it. "It's a good idea, but — "

"But! It's always *but* with you."

" — *but* Robert could just ask the messenger who sent the letter."

"You're right! Phooey! Sometimes I want you to be wrong. You're so sensible. You're always thinking of reasons. It can be really annoying! If you weren't so sensible, we could just mail it to him."

We finally put the letter away for our archives, which were stored in Mia's house for a few weeks.

The next day, I saw Robert ahead of me in the hall between second and third periods. That wasn't so unusual. I always looked for him around second period and then walked behind him. This time, though, all of a sudden, he turned around and looked straight at me.

"I thought he was going to say something," I told Mia when I met her at the end of the day. "And I almost — " I stopped.

"You almost what? *What?*"

"I don't know how to say it. It was like, um, I couldn't breathe. I felt dizzy."

Mia clutched my arm. "He looked right at you? How did he look at you?"

"What do you mean, how? It was a look, the kind of look Robert looks when he looks at you."

"Ami! There are different kinds of looks. Was it a special look? Did he sort of really look right into your eyes, or — "

"No, he didn't look right into my eyes, but you are digging right into my arm. Mia, your hot, sharp little paws!" I pried her fingers loose. "Are you jealous?"

Her face got red. "No!" She looked down. "Yes, I am — a little. Oh, how terrible of me! What a stinker. Jealous of my best friend."

We linked arms and walked along like that for a while. Then I said, "You know what, Mia? You know what I think? When Robert turned around, I think he was actually looking for you."

"Me?"

I nodded. "I'm pretty sure. He looked at me, but — I thought he was disappointed."

106

"Are you just saying that to make me feel good?"

I was, but only a little bit. Mostly, I said it because it was true. "No, he wanted you to be there." As soon as I said it, I felt sort of noble and awful at the same time.

Chapter 15

I visited Mom again over the weekend. It started out okay, but it didn't end that way. We drove up into the mountains to see the leaves. That part was okay, beautiful but sort of boring. Maybe Mom thought so, too. She started yawning, these really huge jaw breakers. Then I started. "It's catching," I said.

"I didn't have that much sleep last night," Mom said.

"How come?"

"Oh, I went to a movie with a friend."

I waited, but she didn't say anything else. It was strange thinking that my mother had friends I didn't know. Was it that Danny who called her the last time I visited? "Late movie?" I said.

"No, not that so much. Just, we got into this

big argument about one of the characters in the movie, and — " She yawned again. "Oh, my! I better get some coffee in the next place we come to."

That was a little mountain village called High Bridge. It was hardly even a village, about a dozen houses, plus a church and a general store. No coffee, so Mom bought a candy bar. "A quick sugar fix." I bought a candy bar, too, and an ice cream sandwich.

"So how's Flower?" Mom said when we got back in the car.

"Who?"

"Your father's little girlfriend."

"Mom. Her name is Forrest. And she's just a friend friend."

"Okay."

"Plus, she's not little. She's taller than Dad. Like you." I don't know why, but my voice went squeaky and weird.

"Ami? Are you feeling sort of worried about your dad and, uh, Forrest?"

I shrugged and bit into the ice cream bar. My throat felt so tight, I didn't think the ice cream would go down.

"Sweetie," Mom said. I was sure she was going to give me a lecture, tell me stuff like I shouldn't panic just because she and Dad had new friends. But all she did was squeeze my hand.

In the next little town, Mom got her coffee and

we toured the Fletcher Museum. It cost fifty cents to go in. It was really somebody's house with all the original Fletcher family's things still in it. There was a cast iron stove in the kitchen and a hole in the floor where they drew up water from the cistern in the cellar.

We went up a narrow staircase. There were three bedrooms with little pine chests and old brass beds covered with quilts. There were old-fashioned dresses hanging on the wall and cracked bowls on the pine chests. Little cards were attached to everything. SOLID CHERRY WOOD DESK, HAND HEWN AND HAND CARVED FOR ABIGAIL FLETCHER, AN ELEVENTH BIRTHDAY PRESENT FROM HER PARENTS. . . . THIS QUILT WAS HAND-MADE FOR ABIGAIL FLETCHER BY HER MOTHER, NANCY MONROE FLETCHER.

It was sad to think of all the people who had lived here and were dead now. Downstairs, in the hall, there were pictures of the Fletcher family. I looked at Abigail Fletcher's picture for a long time. She was wearing old-fashioned clothes and her hair was in long braids tied with white ribbons but, otherwise, she was almost Mia's double. She looked more like Mia than Stacey did. I called my mother. "Mom, look at this. Who does this remind you of?"

She put on her glasses. "Who?"

"It's Mia," I said. "Abigail looks exactly like Mia."

"Does she?" She looked again. "Maybe I've forgotten what Mia looks like."

How could she say that? How could Mom forget what Mia looked like? Was she going to forget what I looked like next?

All the way back to New Castle, going down the twisting mountain roads, I thought about the Fletchers and how their house and all their furniture was still the same, still right where it had always been. If somebody could bring Abigail and her parents back to life today, they could walk into their house, know where everything was, and have everything the way they'd always had it. Then I thought, Mom could do that, too, if she wanted to. We hadn't changed anything. The only thing different in the house was that she wasn't there.

"Mom. When are you going to come home?"

She looked at me, then back at the road. "Ami, it's not my home anymore." When she said that, I wished I hadn't said anything.

That night, right after we ate, Mom opened the couch and made up the bed. "You go ahead and watch TV," she said. "I'm really wiped out, I'm going to sleep, hon."

I sat up late. I'd watch the screen for a while, then I'd fade out, thinking about Abigail Fletcher living in that little house with her parents, writing at a desk her father made for her, sleeping under a quilt her mother made for her. Then I'd remember how Mom said, It's not my home anymore.

I must have fallen asleep, sitting on the edge of the bed. When I opened my eyes, there was

111

a horror movie on TV. A woman was being chased by a mad strangler.

Mom woke up. "Ami, what are you watching?" She looked at it for a few minutes, yawning and rubbing her eyes. "What a disgusting movie! I hate these movies where women are always being shown as the victims. What can people be thinking of when they make this trash?" Then she lay down and went back to sleep. I sat up, watching right to the end, even though I hated it. Then, all night, I had terrifying nightmares.

The next morning it was raining, but we couldn't go out, anyway, because Mom had work to do. She sat cross-legged on the couch with a pile of papers next to her.

I read for a while, then just hung around, looking out the window, wishing it would stop raining and that the time would pass, so I could go home. I was tired, but there was no place to take a nap. I yawned all the way to the bus station.

"Did you get enough sleep, hon?" Mom said.

"I didn't get any sleep." As soon as I said it, I really felt like crying. "I had horrible nightmares all night."

Mom pulled into a parking space. "Was it that awful movie?"

"Yes." I got out of the car and put on my knapsack. "Why did you let me watch it?"

"What do you mean?"

"Just what I said." I walked over to my bus.

Mom came up behind me. "Ami." She grabbed me by the shoulder. "Why did you let yourself watch it?" She pulled me around, right out of the line. "You watched it, I didn't."

"You should have stopped me."

"Why?" she said. "Don't you have any responsibility for yourself?"

"You know why. Because you're my mother! Or have you forgotten that, too?" I pulled away and ran up the steps into the bus.

Chapter 16

I was in a terrible mood for days. I wasn't nice
to anybody, not even Mia — maybe, especially
Mia. Wednesday, we went over to the mall after
school and we couldn't agree on anything. No,
the truth is, *I* couldn't agree on anything. This
is the way the whole afternoon went.

Mia: "Did you see those new shoes in Ed-
ward's? They're adorable. Let's go in and try
them on."

Ami: "Bo-ring!"

Mia: "Oh. Okay, want to check out the
makeup at Flah's?"

Ami: "Blaaaagh."

Mia: "Mmmm. Let's see if the vitamin store is
giving away anything good."

Ami: "Sssss!"

Mia: "We could get some cheese samples at Hickory Farm."

Ami: "Sssssss!"

Mia: "Is there something on your mind?"

Ami: "Huh?"

Mia: "What do you want to do?"

Ami: "Noth-ing!"

Mia: "Want an ice cream cone?"

Ami: "Don't care."

Mia: "I suppose that means yes. I'll buy. Basic chocolate and vanilla today? Or do you want something exotic?"

Ami: "Whatever."

Mia got the cones and we sat down on the railing by the fountain. The grumpier I was to Mia, the grumpier I felt. We always trade cones halfway, but instead of taking her ice cream and giving her mine as usual, I scarfed mine down. It was just a mean thing to do. Mia looked at me and slowly finished her ice cream.

After that, we went into a bookstore to read. We started reading books together in the bookstore a long time ago. We were ten years old and nobody would let us have a copy of a best-selling book called *Her Flaming Wicked Ways*, so we read it in the store, little by little. And we've gone on doing that.

Mia took the book we were reading now (*Beach Towels*), and we sat down behind a table full of marked-down books. But even before she could open to our page, I said, "This is dumb."

"What's dumb?" Mia said. "The book?"

"No! The book is good, but we should buy it if we want to read it. We're not still ten years old. At least, I know I'm not."

"Ami," Mia said, "are you mad at me or something?"

"Or something," I said, in a very sarcastic way. I didn't know I was going to say it like that.

Mia got up and put the book back on the shelf. Then she came back to me and said very, very quietly, in a voice just like her father's, "I'll tell you something, Ami. I'm not talking to you again, until you get out of your negative mood."

"That suits me fine," I said.

And Mia said in that same quiet, quiet voice, "If you don't get out of that negative mood, I might never talk to you again."

"Excellent," I said, even more sarcastic than before.

So then we left. We rode the bus to Mia's stop without saying a word to each other. When Mia got off, I pretended to be looking out the window.

The next day in school, we still weren't talking. After school, I went down to the gym to practice an exercise I read about in the newspaper. You get up on a box or a chair, jump down into a crouch, and then immediately jump into the air. That's all, but it's supposed to improve your reflexes, especially for basketball

116

jump shots. I did that for a while, then I hung around shooting baskets with Bunny Larrabee, until the custodian told us to leave.

At home, there were two notes on the bulletin board, a long one from Dad and a short one from Fred. Dad's note said, *Kids, I'm eating supper with Forrest.* Then all about what we should eat and how it was my turn to do the dishes, et cetera, et cetera. At the bottom, he wrote, *See you later. Dad.*

Fred's note said, *Out with Bill. Back early. Fred.*

"Thanks a lot, everybody," I said. First the fight with Mia, now nobody home. I opened a box of coconut spirals and started eating. I ate them all, with a quart of milk. I felt sort of sick after that, so I drank the rest of a can of peach nectar and ate a couple of apples. Then I felt sicker, and I still had to feed Alcott his slimy, smelly, raw liver.

I threw the meat down on a piece of newspaper. "Why don't you become a vegetarian like Bill?" I yelled. Poor Alcott. He sort of slunk over to his meat and just licked it for a moment, looking up at me to see if I was going to yell again.

I refused to even look at the dishes. Maybe I'd wash them later. And maybe I wouldn't. Maybe I'd just leave a note. *Fred and Dad, I'm not washing any more dishes. We need a dishwasher. And I don't mean me.*

Unccy and I walked around for a while. I clattered down the stairs and up again. I can't do that when Dad is home, because he's always correcting papers or making up tests, and he says loud noises destroy his concentration. "Tooo baaad for you, Daaaad." Clatter. Clatter. Clatter. Then I went into my parents' room and walked across their bed with my shoes on. It was like being mean to Mia. It made me feel better, in a kind of awful way.

"Sweetheart, you're in such a bad mood," Unccy Bernard said. "Tssst. Poor Ami. Some days, it seems like everything goes wrong. They all just go off and leave you . . . and your best friend doesn't want to speak to you. Tsssst!"

We went downstairs into the kitchen. "And they always expect me to do the dishes." I wiped my eyes on his fur.

"Dishes! Tishes! Fishes! Who cares about the dishes!" Unccy put his paws to his forehead. "My little sweetheart, you tell Daddy everybody has to wash their own dishes."

"Okay, Unccy." My voice wobbled.

"You need me to take care of you. Next time you visit Momma, you take me with you. You won't even notice I'm there. I'll sleep with you and Momma. Or maybe I'll sleep in the sink."

"I wouldn't let you sleep in the sink."

"Well, my little sweetheart, a sink can be very comfortable if you're the right size. Put in a little pillow and you've got a bed."

Just then the phone rang. I was sure it was Mia to make up. "Hello! Mia?" I said.

118

"Ami?"

"Mom?"

"It's your mom."

"I know."

"You sounded a little unsure." She laughed.

"I knew who you were."

"Well . . . how are you?"

"Okay," I said.

"Okay? Or good? Or really good?"

"Okay."

"Ah. Just okay?"

"Uh-huh."

"I've been thinking about you all week."

I sat down on the cupboard and clipped the phone against my shoulder. "You have?"

"I always think about you."

"You do?"

"I think about you a lot."

I don't know why, but I started crying. And then Mom started crying, too.

"Oh, oh, we have to stop this," Mom said, in a really weepy voice. "Ami? Are you still there? What I really called about — we didn't part too happily on the weekend, did we?"

"I guess not."

"I hope you didn't let it get to you."

I said, "No," but my voice went all funny.

"Oh, honey! That's what I was afraid of. I think we had a bad misunderstanding. I'm really sorry, I shouldn't have let you get on the bus until we talked it out."

"That's the only bus I could take."

Mom sniffled. "My practical little duckling. I could have driven you home."

"Then you would have been tired the next day."

"Who cares? I don't want us to be unhappy with each other."

"I hate fights."

"I know, sweetie, but listen, people fight all the time. The thing is, if you, underneath, love each other, then it's okay, you make it up and go on from there."

"I guess so."

"You know I love you, don't you, honey?"

"I guess so."

"No! No guessing. That is a fact of life. That is something that will never change."

"You loved Daddy, too. Did you think that would never change?"

"Oh." She went silent. Then she said, "Yes. I did think we would love each other forever. But that doesn't make me wrong about you. The love I have for you is entirely different."

"Why? What if it isn't?"

"Oh, but it is, Ami. The way I love you — nothing in the world can shake that."

"Nothing? What if you decided you didn't like me?"

Mom laughed. "Why shouldn't I like you?"

"You don't have to like me just because I'm your kid. I'm not always a very nice person."

"Oh, come on, you are."

"No, I'm not. I can be mean and sarcastic. I can be really nasty, I'm not kidding."

She was quiet for a moment, then she said, "Well. Even if you are a mean person — which I don't think for a minute — even so, I still love you and I always will. A lot of things change, but not that."

"Why does *anything* have to change?"

"That's like asking why do leaves fall."

"It's sad."

"Sweetie, life is sometimes sad. . . . I love you a whole lot, Ami."

"I love you, too, Mom," I said.

Then we hung up.

Chapter 17

Unccy was sitting on the bureau, watching me brush my hair. "Unccy says, being friends with your friends is always better than being enemies with your friends."

"It's not so bad to fight if, underneath, you love each other."

"True, my little sweetheart. But fights are fights and making up is making uppp . . . ooof!" Unccy flopped over.

I picked him up. "I'm not mad at Mia anymore."

"That's my little sweetheart." Unccy patted my face.

I nodded. I knew just what I was going to say when I saw Mia in school. *Sorry, Mia, sorry I was such a beast.*

You sure were, Ami! A dog!
A snake.
A rat!
Why are we insulting all these animals?

Then we'd laugh and squeeze hands and everything would be just the way it always was. But when I saw her just before homeroom, she walked past me and didn't say anything. So I didn't say anything, either. That was Thursday. Friday was even worse. I saw Mia in the cafeteria, sitting with Bunny Larrabee. They were talking and laughing. Bunny waved, but Mia didn't even look my way.

That night, Dad was making supper. He always cooks spaghetti on Friday nights; he did it even when Mom was home. "Who's washing the dishes?" he said, while he stirred the sauce. "Ami?" Nobody had done them for a couple of days. The sink was loaded and there were dishes all over the cupboard.

"Why me, Dad?"

"Best reason in the world. You're here."

"We need a dishwasher."

"Can't afford it."

"How much does it cost?"

"Ami, take my word for it, child power is cheaper."

"I have to be in a really good mood to wash dishes."

"That's a new, improved excuse. Get thee to the sink, Cinderella."

I did about half of the dishes, and all the time I was thinking about Mia and me and feeling worse and worse. Finally I stopped. "Dad? I don't really want to do this."

"What's the matter, Ami? You think it's child abuse?"

I flung down the scrubber. "Do you think everything's a joke?"

Dad looked at me. There was a little tomato sauce on his lips. He likes to taste as he cooks. "I didn't realize we were being serious."

"Now you do! Why can't I leave the rest of the dishes for Fred? I never see him do dishes. Why is it always my job?" I didn't know I was going to say all that. I really surprised myself.

Dad sighed. "Gimme a break, will you, Ami? It's Friday, end of a long week. Does it matter who does the dishes? We're supposed to all be pulling together here."

Suddenly I thought of something else. "Did you tell Mom she couldn't take me with her?"

"Take you where? Is she going on a trip?"

"No, I mean when she left — " I was going to say home, then I remembered Mom saying, That's not my home anymore. " — when she went to live in New Castle. Did you say you wouldn't let me go?"

"Oh, that. Yes."

"Are you sorry now?"

"In general, no. At this very moment, yes!"

"Thanks a lot."

"Ami. Another joke." He hugged me.

After that, I took the phone into the dining room, closed the kitchen door, and called Mia.

"Hello?" she said.

"This is Ami."

"Oh. Hello."

"Hello. What are you doing?"

"Taking care of Sara."

"She's cute."

"What are you doing?"

"Not much. Fighting with my father. And I just finished washing a truckload of dishes."

"Well, Sara's crying. I better go."

"Okay."

"Bye."

"Bye."

I put the phone down carefully and stood there staring at it. I tried to make up with Mia, and what did she do? Nothing. Got off the phone as quick as she could. *Sara's crying.* What a lie. She just didn't want to talk to me. *I better go. Bye.* Nothing else to say to me. *Bye.* Well, that was all right with me. Now I knew the truth, anyway. She didn't care about me at all.

Fred came in from outside and dumped his books on the couch. He looked at me. "What are you doing, praying over that phone?"

"Fred, did you ever have a fight with Jan and then try to make up and she didn't want to?"

"Yeah, I've made her really mad sometimes."

"What'd you do?"

"To make her mad? I don't know. Stuff. She says sometimes I don't hear her talking, things like that."

"You don't listen to her? Why not?"

"Did I say that? I listen to her. Just, sometimes, maybe I'm thinking of something else. Then she starts steaming, and when Jan steams, you can about see the algebraic signs coming out of her ears. Is Dad working on supper?" He went into the kitchen.

The phone rang. Maybe it was Jan, calling Fred. I let it ring. Maybe it was Bill, saying he wanted to come over and play his guitar. Another ring. Or Robert. He'd decided he was madly in love with me. "Ami," Dad called, "get the phone, will you?" I let it ring two more times, then I picked it up. "Pelter residence."

"Ami? Hi. I'm not taking care of Sara anymore."

"Excellent."

"When you called before, I thought you wanted to make up."

I started to say something sarcastic. *What a brilliant deduction! How did you ever figure that out!* I began to feel really bad. I couldn't even speak.

"Ami? Ami, do you want to make up?"

"Do you want to?"

"I want to, Ami, if you want to. Do you want to?"

"Not if you're going to hang up on me."

"Ami, I couldn't help it. Sara was bawling her head off."

"Is that the truth?"

"Yes! Word of honor! I swear on my mother's grave."

"Your mother isn't dead."

"Well, if she was, I'd swear on her grave. You want me to kill her, so I can prove it to you?"

"Oh, ugh, that's terrible."

"I know, it's awful! It's sick."

"And your mother is so nice."

"No, she isn't. She's only nice to you. She's bizarre! She nags me all the time. She never leaves me alone. I always have to take care of Sara. Which is her work."

"I want to see you," I said.

"Can I come over now?"

"Come for supper. You want to come for supper?"

Mia came over about twenty minutes later. We hugged each other and kissed. I said our fight was my fault and Mia said, "Who cares! I missed you." Then we hugged again and danced around the room until Fred yelled for us to come into the kitchen for supper.

Dad makes great spaghetti; that and pancakes are his two best dishes. "This is fabulous, Mr. Pelter," Mia said, and Dad tried to look modest.

After supper, Mia said she and I would wash the dishes. "Won't we, Ami?" I should have said no and made Fred do them, but I was so happy we'd made up, I would have washed ten times as many dishes. We went a little crazy after Dad and Fred left. First, too much detergent. Then we knocked into each other and splashed water over everything.

"We'll have to wash the floor," I said.

"And hang ourselves out to dry!"

Every dumb little thing we said made us laugh.

"You know what?" Mia said. "We should do something special to celebrate."

I dried a plate and tried to think what it could be. We'd had ice cream for dessert. "We could make taffy," I said.

"Not food," Mia said. "Something better." She dipped a glass into the sudsy water. "I know. Let's call Robert." And she got a great big smile on her face.

Chapter 18

"You dial," Mia said.

"But you talk. Remember, first you ask for Robert, then when he gets on, you say, 'Is this Robert Smith?' "

Mia leaned on my shoulder. "How many times should we let it ring?"

"Hello?" a woman said.

I pushed the phone at Mia.

"Can I, um, speak to, Robert?"

I leaned in close so I could hear.

"Hello?" Robert said.

"Hello, Robert?"

"Yeah."

Mia looked at me. "Robert? Hi. This is Mia," she said. I couldn't believe it. She patted her mouth like she was trying not to burst out laughing.

"Mia?" Robert said, like there were at least forty-two Mia's in our school.

"Mia Jenson."

"Oh."

"I'm, uh, here with my friend, Ami."

"Who?"

"Ami Pelter. She says hi, too."

"You mean Foghorn Ami?"

"Yes," I whispered hoarsely.

"That's not very nice," Mia said, rolling her eyes at me.

"No offense," Robert said. "They call me Carrot Top."

"Your hair is beautiful."

I couldn't believe she'd had the nerve to say it. Suddenly, she stuck the phone out to me, right next to my mouth. "Talk!" she whispered.

"Hi," I said. I mean, I croaked. I sounded just like a frog.

"Hi."

"This is Foghorn Ami."

"This is Carrot Top."

Then I didn't have anything else to say, so I gave the phone back to Mia. "Hi, it's me, again," she said.

"Me, Mia? So, what are you doing, me Mia?"

"Talking to you."

"That's humorous."

"What are you doing?" Mia looked over at me,

sticking out her tongue and making faces like she was dying.

"I'm going out to play basketball."

"Where?"

"In the driveway. We have a light out there."

"We have a hoop in our driveway, too. So does Ami."

"Do you like to play basketball?"

"No, I don't like sports much. I'm terrible at them, anyway. My sister Stacey is good. And so is Ami."

"I know," he said. "I saw her playing in gym. I saw you, too."

"You did?"

"Yeah. Well, I have to go now. Bye."

"Bye. Ami says bye, too."

"Bye, Ami."

I leaned into the phone. "Bye, Robert."

"Bye, Ami. Bye Mia."

"Bye bye, Robert," we both said. Then we hung up.

"I don't know how you did that," I said.

"I know! Do you believe me? I didn't even think, I just did it."

"Hello, Robert, this is Mia," I said.

Mia leaned against me. "He's so nice," she said. "Wasn't he sweet, Ami?"

Chapter 19

Saturday morning. Big chores day. Fred and Dad had divided up the shopping and errands. I was stuck with the vacuuming. I did the downstairs, then I couldn't stand it anymore. I'd rather wash a bathtub full of dishes than drag the vacuum cleaner around the house.

I went outside to shoot baskets. It was cold, there'd been a frost last night, and the grass was still white.

"Hi, Ami," someone said. It was Bill. He had his guitar slung over his back. He was wearing a white knit fisherman's sweater and the curved silver earring. He looked really nice. "Is Fred around?"

"No. He's doing errands."

"Do you know when he'll be back?"

"Maybe not for a while."

"I'll wait." He put his guitar down. "Want to play one-on-one?"

We played for about half an hour. Bill would make these great leaps, shoot, and the ball would either bang against the backboard or bounce on the rim and come flying off. He just laughed. "I give up. I'm leaving basketball to you, Ami."

I looked at my watch. I should go in and finish the vacuuming. Or would that be rude? "Well, I guess I'll go in," I said.

"You're going in?"

"Uh-huh." I dribbled the ball. "I have to do some things, but you can wait for Fred."

"Out here?"

"Sure, that's okay."

"So when did you say Fred would be back?"

"It might be a while." Maybe I could vacuum the upstairs fast and then come out again and talk to Bill.

"Ahh, Ami." Bill stood up. "It's pretty cold out here." He pointed to his head. "Notice? Left ear, turning red?"

I was embarrassed. I should have told him he could wait inside. "Oh! Come on in, I'm sorry, I thought — "

Bill followed me into the house. "I don't mind the cold for myself, Ami. But my guitar, he's a sensitive lad. If he gets too cold, he won't play nice for me."

We went into the living room. Some blankets were rumpled up at one end of the couch. I pushed them out of the way. "Well, um, sit down." I was still holding the basketball.

"Do you sing, Ami?"

"Just in chorus, in school.'"

"You ever try singing solo?"

I shook my head and looked around for someplace to put the basketball.

"You should try it. From your speaking voice, it sounds like you might have a really special singing voice."

"Some people call me Foghorn Ami."

"Yeah?" Bill tuned his guitar. He strummed a few chords. "I have a song I just wrote, that's why I came over. I wanted to play it for someone. You want to work on it with me?"

"Me? How?"

"Can you read music?"

"A little." Maybe I could drop the basketball into the magazine basket. "I took piano lessons for a while when I was younger."

"Why'd you stop?"

"They were sort of expensive and, you know, I wasn't that good."

"Did you like piano?"

I nodded.

"There. You see. You should have gone on." He tightened a string. "I don't know how people live without music. Sit down." He patted the couch next to him.

I sat down. I was still holding the basketball.

Bill took a sheet of music paper out of his pocket and unfolded it. "Now, see, this is the song I wrote. I'll sing it for you. Just for the words, first. We'll work on the phrasing and stuff after we've got the words down."

The song was about a girl "with a sad little face" who worked in a pizza place, and how he used to watch her and think about talking to her. Then he stopped going there for a while, and when he went back, she was gone and nobody knew where, or what had happened to her. "Looking for the girl . . . looking all over for the one I used to see in Dom's Pizza Place," he sang. "Hey! Oh, hey! Why didn't I tell her, why didn't I say. . . . Babe, it's okay. . . . Yeah, it's okay, it's okay. . . ."

"So, what do you think?" he said.

"I like it."

"Yeah? You do?" Bill pulled his guitar around and bent over it. "Not a whole lot, though, huh?"

I was really surprised. He sounded so unsure of himself. I didn't think he was like that at all. "No. I love it. I think it's wonderful."

"Oh. Really?" He smiled.

"Is it true? I mean, the girl — "

"Sure, she worked in Dom's Pizza. You know the place I mean, on the Boulevard?"

"Were you in love with her?"

"Liked her a whole lot, but just like the song says, I never even talked to her."

"Why not?"

He struck a couple of chords. "Too . . . shy
. . . ." He raised his eyebrows at me. "I . . .
confess. . . ."

"You should have taken your guitar."

"Hey, that's smart," he said. "That's the only
time — how did you know?"

I shrugged. I was embarrassed the way he was
looking at me, but I liked it, too. "I know some
things," I said.

"You sure do." He ruffled my hair. "Okay.
Let's you, me, and that basketball do some singing here."

Chapter 20

"You should do your nails, Ami," Mia said.

"These things?" I never took care of my nails and I didn't like them long.

Mia held out her hands to show me her fingernails. She'd painted them a bluey red. "I did my toes, too. I like it, even if my mother does say it's a primitive ritual."

It was the day before Thanksgiving recess, when our school always goes on a picnic to Enoch Falls Park. Three years ago on picnic day, it snowed. Everybody packed into the buses, anyway, and drove to the park. Our principal, Mrs. Giordono, has a picture in her office of people eating their hot dogs with mittens on.

This year, the sun was shining, there wasn't

137

a cloud around. The sky was the same color as Mia's sweater. She looked even prettier than usual.

Mr. Cooper yelled through a megaphone for anybody who wanted to play softball to meet over on the diamond. "I'm going over," I said. "What are you going to do?"

"I don't know. I'll find something."

"You could play softball."

"Me?"

"Well . . . I don't really have to play."

Mia gave me a push. "I know this is going to come as a shock, but I can exist for an hour without you, Ami."

"Okay, then. Bye!" I ran toward the diamond.

"Ami Pelter. Good." Mr. Cooper waved me over to one side. "You play outfield for the Enoch Fallers."

"Good old Coop. He always has to have cute team names," somebody grumbled in my ear. It was Miles Hammond, Robert's friend. He had a scowl on his face.

"Good old Miles," I said, "you always have to have a scowl." It just popped out.

I thought he'd be mad, but, instead, he laughed. "Good old Ami, always there with the truth."

"At least I made you smile."

"At least I made you talk."

Then Mr. Cooper blew his whistle and the game started.

The game was still going on when Mia came over to where I was playing outfield. "Ami! I need you. Come here!"

"Mia — " A ball bounced across the field toward me. Everyone yelled and screamed. I ran, putting out my mitt, fell, but somehow caught the ball and threw it in.

"Yaaay, Ami," Miles cheered. That was nice. When he got up to bat and made a base hit, I clapped for him.

The minute the game was over, Mia pulled me away. "I did something! You have to help me. I put a note in Robert's pocket."

"In his pocket?"

"Don't ask me why I did it! The idea came to me and I did it. It was so easy, Ami. I walked by him casually and slipped the note in his pocket."

"What did you write?"

" 'Meet us at two o'clock, at the cave on the red trail, for a special surprise.' "

"What's the surprise?"

"I don't know! We'll figure something out."

"Did you sign the note?"

"You mean, my name? I'm not that far gone."

"Mia, why'd you pick the red trail?"

"Does it make any difference? Maybe because red is for love."

"It's the longest trail in the park, Mia."

She waved her hand. "Trifles, trifles. What are we going to do, Ami? Just go there, or what?"

I thought about it. "How do we know he's even read the note?"

"Because I watched him. He put his hands in his pockets, he found the note, and then he read it."

"Well, if you didn't sign it, maybe we don't have to do anything."

"I did sign it. I wrote, 'Two people who love you.'" Her face was pink. "What do we do now, Ami?"

"Eat. I'm hungry." I went over to the table where I'd left my lunchbag and took out my sandwiches. I ate one and put one in my pocket.

Mrs. Giordono walked by us, her arms full of bags of marshmallows. "Going to join the marshmallow roast, girls?"

"In a couple minutes," Mia said politely. "So?" She shook my arm. "What are we going to *do*?"

"Let's watch Robert to see what he does. Only we can't let him know we're watching him."

"Okay," Mia said, "we hang out near him and act natural. But we better have a signal, like waving a scarf or something."

"If we stick together, Mia, we won't need a signal."

Mia sighed. "I know, but it would be so much fun to wave a scarf mysteriously."

We looked around for Robert. "Having a good time, girls?" Dad said. He and Ms. Linsley were refereeing a checkers tournament. We finally spotted Robert near the playground with Alex and Miles. They were eating hamburgers and passing around a bag of chips. We hid in the trees and watched.

"Robert's so cute," Mia whispered.

"Miles is nice, too."

"The fat boy?"

"Mia, you always say that. There's more to Miles than his shape."

A gang of kids came swinging through the woods. We picked up some leaves and pretended to be studying them. Robert, Alex, and Miles were still standing around, eating and talking. Then they strolled over to the swings. Alex stood up on a swing. Miles and Robert sat down, hanging on to the chains. They were still talking. Then they went over and scuffed around in the sandbox and talked some more.

"They sure talk a lot," I said.

"Maybe they're talking about us!" Mia shivered.

"What if Robert guessed who sent the note?" Mia pinched my arm hard. "Ami! Look!"

Robert was walking away from the other two. We followed him, but stayed in the woods. He cut across the field and went into the men's bathroom. That was embarrassing. We walked away, but not too far.

When he came out, Robert didn't go back to the playground. He went straight toward the red trail.

Chapter 21

The red trail went past the falls, twisted around into a different part of the woods, and came out below the falls. We tried to stay far enough behind Robert so he wouldn't hear us. The woods were really quiet. No birds, just a few squirrels.

"Shhhh!" Mia said. "Your feet sound like thunder."

"Oh, pardon me, Chief Light Foot, I forgot my moccasins."

"Ami, you think it's all right to criticize me, but when I say anything — "

"What are you talking about, Mia? When did I criticize you?"

"When? Always! Just a little while ago, you told me not to call Miles the fat boy."

"Mia, I only said — "

"I know what you said."

We came around a turn in the trail, arguing, not looking, and there was Robert, waiting for us. "I knew it was you two," he said.

We all just looked at each other for a minute, then Robert said, "So what's my big surprise, Ami?"

Why was he asking me? I didn't know any more than he did.

"This is your surprise." Mia took him by the arms and kissed him the way we kissed when we made up our quarrels, first on one cheek and then on the other. Robert really looked surprised and he blushed. He took off his glasses and hooked them over his shirt.

Mia and I looked at each other and she wriggled her eyebrows to remind me of that morning in the Bagel Tree. *I remember!* I wriggled back.

She poked me. "Your turn." For a minute, I didn't get it. Then I did. I was supposed to kiss Robert, too. I leaned toward him and kissed him on the cheek. He smelled really nice, his cheek was soft, but sort of firm, too.

The next thing I knew, he kissed me back on the cheek. And then, he kissed Mia on the lips! It was a real kiss. They put their arms around each other and kissed, just the way Jan and Fred had that time in the kitchen. Well, I thought, even if I'm not kissing, I'm getting plenty of experience watching.

After that, we all walked back together, talking

about the picnic, the food, the teachers, stuff like that. Robert said, "Mr. Pelter is okay. He's kind of boring sometimes."

"That's Ami's father," Mia said.

"Ami's father?" He really blushed, more than he did when we kissed him. "I didn't know that. I thought it was just — you know — the same name."

"I don't care that you said that. I mean, my father has to be something, so he's an English teacher."

"My father's an electrical contractor," Mia said.

"I know that, Mia."

"I wasn't telling you, Ami! I was telling Robert. I might want to be an electrician," she said. "I'm telling Robert, Ami. Got it? It's a good trade and there aren't many women electricians, my father says, so I'd be a trailblazer. Which sounds neat. But it might be more fun to work on a newspaper."

"What do you want to do?" I said to Robert.

"I don't know. Maybe something in television."

"I know someone who works in radio. Harley Juster."

"The DJ? You know him?" He acted impressed and I promised to show him Harley Juster's autograph.

When we got back to the picnic, Robert went to find his friends. The picnic was almost over, but we had to police up the park before we left.

144

I dumped a can into a plastic bag and thought about all the things that had changed since school started. Just three months and so many things were different. Fred getting ready to go to France in the spring. Dad and Forrest. And really knowing now that Mom wasn't coming back home. Only Mia and I were the same. Or were we?

We sat together on the bus going home. Ms. Linsley was our bus monitor. She stood up in front of the bus and led us in songs. ". . . and the wiiide mouth frog said. . . ."

Davis Buck looked over at me as I was singing and snickered. I remembered what Bill had said about my voice. I looked out the window. "Rootie tootie," I hummed, and I felt this little stirring inside me, this fluttering like a mouse inside my chest, a tiny, nibbly feeling. I didn't know what it was, I only knew what it wasn't. It wasn't sadness, it wasn't fear.

Coming back into the city we passed the old railroad station, rows of little houses, a brick church. A kid in a window waved. I waved back. And there was that stirring inside me again, that nibbly fluttering, as if something were going to happen, something good, something interesting. But what? *What was it?* Then, just for a moment, I thought I knew. I understood. It was *everything*, it was my whole life, it was all the things that were going to happen to me that hadn't happened yet.

Chapter 22

"I don't believe it," Mia said for about the fourth time. "I just don't believe it."

"Well, do you like it?"

She looked at me in the mirror over my bureau. "I don't know."

Last night I had cut my hair. Strands of hair had fallen all over the floor, long strands of hair I'd grown for almost thirteen years.

"I'm still in shock," Mia said. "We look so different now! You with your short hair and me with my long hair."

"We never looked the same, Mia."

"I know, it's just — it's so *different*."

I picked up the scissors and snipped the air. "I didn't know I was going to do it. I didn't plan it, I just did it. I took a shower and washed my hair, and — you know how good the shower

146

makes you feel? That's the way I felt. I was singing this song a friend of mine wrote — "

"What song?" Mia said. "What friend?"

"A friend of Fred's."

"You mean Jan? She wrote a song?"

"No, not Jan. Someone else."

"Who? What's her name?"

"His name. Bill."

"Who's he? What's he got to do with cutting your hair? You know what? When I walked in, I almost didn't recognize you."

"I know, it's so funny. I keep looking at myself. Is that Ami? Remember how you wrote the note to Robert? Just did it? That's the way I cut my hair." I opened my bureau drawer and showed her an envelope. "I put some of my hair in here. Maybe my mom will want it."

"What'd your father say?"

"He didn't see it yet."

"Well . . . I think I like it," Mia said.

"You do? Honestly?" I was relieved. I went to the window and pulled up the shade. Just this morning, it had started snowing.

Mia sat down on the bed. "It makes you look almost like someone else." A little smile came and went on her face. "Ami, now that you've cut your hair — I know this sounds stupid, but I'm going to tell you something."

"What — are you going to cut your hair, too?"

"No. Not that. Robert and I went to the movies."

"You and Robert? When?"

"Last week. Last Saturday."

I sat down on the bed next to her. "Last Saturday, when I went to visit my mother?"

Mia nodded. "He called up and we were talking, and he said what did I do on Saturdays? And I said when Ami's not around, not so much, it was pretty boring."

"Did you say that, really?"

"Well, it's true. I said maybe I'd go to the mall or something. And he said he was going over to the mall to see a movie. So then I said was it a good movie? And he said he thought so, and did I want to meet him there and go, too?"

"You sat together?"

She nodded.

"Was it fun? Or what?"

"Not exactly fun. Not the way I have fun with you. . . . He put his arm around me. Are you mad?"

"I know you and Robert like each other."

"Ami." She looked at me seriously. "Just because I like Robert, I don't want it to change us. I'll always love you."

I hugged her. "I'll always love you, Mia."

After a moment, she got the scissors. "Want me to fix your hair up a little? You didn't get it so good in back."

I sat there, with my eyes closed, listening to the little crackle of the scissors and that other quiet sound, of snow falling, that's hardly a sound at all.

148

"There," Mia said. "See if you like it." I looked in the mirror. Mia looked over my shoulder. "We should take a picture."

I got Dad's camera. It has a setting on it so you can take your own picture. I set the camera up on the bureau, then ran and stood with Mia in front of the window. Our arms were linked, our heads together.

"Cheese, Ami! Say cheese, Amikins!"

"Cheese. Cheese, Miaseea!"

About the Author

NORMA FOX MAZER is the author of more than twenty books for young readers, among them the Newbery honor winner *After the Rain*, as well as *Taking Terri Mueller*, *When We First Met*, and *Downtown*. Ms. Mazer has twice won the Lewis Carroll Shelf Award; she has also won the California Young Reader Medal and has been nominated for the National Book Award.

A, My Name Is Ami is a companion book to *B, My Name Is Bunny*; *C, My Name Is Cal*; *D, My Name Is Danita*; and *E, My Name Is Emily*, all published by Scholastic.

Ms. Mazer lives with her husband, author Harry Mazer, in the Pompey Hills outside Syracuse, New York.

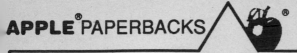